Gold from Crete

C. S. FORESTER

SPHERE BOOKS LIMITED
30/32 Gray's Inn Road, London WC1X 8JL

First published by Michael Joseph Ltd 1971
Copyright © Dorothy E. Forester 1971
First Sphere Books edition 1978

Set in Intertype Baskerville

Printed in Great Britain by
Hunt Barnard Printing Ltd.,
Aylesbury, Bucks.

Contents

Gold from Crete

The officers of H.M.S. *Apache* were sizing up the Captain D. at the same time that he was doing the same to them. A Captain D. – captain commanding destroyers – was a horrible nuisance on board if, as in this case, the ship in which he elected – or was compelled by circumstances – to hoist his distinguishing pendant was not fitted as a flotilla leader. The captain needed cabin space himself, and he brought with him a quartet of staff officers who also needed cabin space. Physically, that meant that four out of the seven officers already on board the *Apache* would be more uncomfortable than usual, and in a destroyer that meant a great deal. More than that; morally, the effect was still more profound. It meant that with a captain on board, even if he tried not to interfere with the working of the ship, the commander and the other officers, and the lower deck ratings as well, for the matter of that, felt themselves under the scrutiny of higher authority. The captain's presence would introduce something of the atmosphere of a big ship, and it would undoubtedly cut short the commander's pleasure in his independent command.

So Commander Hammett and his officers eyed Captain Crowe and his staff, when they met on the scorching iron deck of the *Apache* in Alexandria Harbour, without any appearance of hospitality. They saw a big man, tall and a little inclined to bulk, who moved with a freedom and ease that hinted at a concealed athleticism. His face was tanned so deeply that it was impossible to guess at his complexion, but under the thick black brows there were a pair of grey eyes that twinkled irrepressibly. They knew his record, of course – much of it was to be read in the rows of coloured ribbon on his chest. There was the D.S.O. he had won as a midshipman at Zeebrugge in 1918 – before Sub-lieutenant Chesterfield had been born – and they knew that they had only to look up the official account of that action to find exactly what Crowe had done there; but everyone knew that midshipmen do not receive D.S.O.s for nothing. The spot of silver that twinkled on the red-and-blue ribbon told of the bar he had received for the part he had played at Narvik last year – not to many men is it given to be decorated for distinguished services twenty-two years apart and still to be hardly entering on middle age. There was the red ribbon that one or two of them recognised as the Bath, and a string of other gay colours that ended in the Victory and General Service ribbons of the last war.

The introductions were brief – most of the officers had at least a nodding acquaintance with one another already. Commander Hammett presented his first lieutenant, Garland, and the other officers down to Sub-lieutenants Chesterfield and Lord Edward Mortimer, R.N.V.R. – this last was a fattish and untidy man in the late thirties whose yachting experience had miraculously brought him out of Mayfair drawing rooms and dropped him on the hard steel deck of the *Apache* – and Crowe indicated his flotilla gunnery officer and navigating officer and signals officer and secretary.

'We will proceed as soon as convenient, Commander,' said Crowe, issuing his first order.

'Aye aye, sir,' said Hammett, as twenty generations of seamen had answered before him. But at least the age of consideration given to omens had passed; it did not occur to Hammett to ponder on the significance of the fact that Crowe's first order had been one of action.

'Get yourselves below and sort yourselves out,' said Crowe to his staff, and as they disappeared he walked forward and ran lightly up to the bridge.

Hammett gave his orders – Crowe was glad to note that he did so without even a side glance out of the tail of his eye at the captain at the end of the bridge – and the ship broke into activity. In response to one order, the yeoman of signals on the bridge bellowed an incomprehensible string of words down to the signal bridge. It passed through Crowe's mind that yeomen of signals were always as incomprehensible as railway porters calling out the names of stations in England, but the signal rating below understood what was said to him, which was all that mattered. A string of coloured flags ran up the halyards, and a moment later yeoman of signals was bellowing the replies received. The flagship gave permission to proceed; the fussy tug out there by the anti-submarine net began to pull open the gate. The bow was pulled in, the warps cast off. The telegraph rang, the propeller began to turn, and the *Apache* trembled a little as she moved away. Everything was done as competently as possible; the simple operation was a faint indication that Crowe would not have to worry about the *Apache* in action, but could confine his attention to the handling of his whole flotilla of twelve destroyers, if and when he should ever succeed in gathering them all together.

A movement just below him caught his attention. The anti-aircraft lookouts were being relieved. At the .50-calibre gun here on the starboard side a burly seaman was taking over the earphones and the glasses. He was a huge man, but all Crowe could see of him, besides his huge bulk and the top of his cap, was his cropped red hair and a wide expanse of neck and ear, burned a solid brick-red from the Mediterranean sun. Then there were a pair of thick wrists covered with dense red hair, and two vast hands that held the glasses as they swept back and forth, back and forth, over the sky from horizon to zenith in ceaseless search for hostile planes. At that moment there were six seamen employed on that task in different parts of the deck, and so exacting was the work that a quarter of an hour every hour was all that could be asked of any man.

Commander Hammett turned at that moment and caught the captain's eye.

'Sorry to intrude on you like this, Hammett,' said Crowe.

'No intrusion at all, sir. Glad to have you, of course.'

Hammett could hardly say anything else, poor devil, thought Crowe, before he went on : 'Must be a devilish nuisance being turned out of your cabin, all the same.'

'Not nearly as much nuisance as to the other officers, sir,' said Hammett. 'When we're at sea I never get aft to my sleeping cabin at all. Turn in always in my sea cabin.'

Perfectly true, thought Crowe. No destroyer captain would think of ever going more than one jump from the bridge at sea.

'Nice of you to spare my feelings,' said Crowe, with a grin. It had to be said in just the right way – Crowe could guess perfectly well at Hammett's resentment at his presence.

'Not at all, sir,' said Hammett briefly.

Sub-lieutenant Chesterfield gave a fresh course to the quartermaster at this moment and changed the conversation.

They were clear of the minefields now and almost out of sight of the low shore. The myriad Levantine spies would have a hard time to guess whither they were bound.

'We'll be in visual touch with the flotilla at dawn, sir,' said Hammett.

'Thank you. I'll let you know if there's any change of plan,' replied Crowe.

He ran down the naked steel ladder to the deck, and walked aft, past the quadruple torpedo tubes and the two pairs of 4.7's towering above him. On the blast screen a monkey sat and gibbered at him, gesticulating with withered little hands. Crowe hated monkeys; he liked dogs and could tolerate cats; he had been shipmates with pets of all species from goats to baby hippopotamuses, but monkeys were his abomination. He hated the filthy little things, their manners and their habits. He ignored this one stolidly as he walked past it to the accompaniment of screamed monkey obscenities. If he were in command of this destroyer he would have seen to it that the little beast did not remain long on board to plague him; as it was, he thought ruefully to himself, as he was in the immeasurably higher position of commanding a flotilla, he would have to endure its presence for fear of hurting the feelings of those under his command.

Down below, Paymaster-Lieutenant Scroggs, his secretary, was waiting for him in the day cabin. Scroggs was looking through a mass of message forms – intercepted wireless messages which gave, when pieced together, a vague and shadowy picture of the progress of the fighting in Crete.

'I don't like the looks of it at all, sir,' said Scroggs.

Neither did Crowe, but he could see no possible good in saying so. His hearty and sanguine temperament could act on bad news, but refused to dwell on it. He had digested the contents of those messages long ago, and he had no desire to worry himself with them again.

'We'll know more about it when we get there,' he said cheerfully. 'I shan't want you for a bit, Scroggs.'

Scroggs acted on the hint and left the cabin, while Crowe sat himself at the table and drew the notepaper to him and began his Thursday letter:

My dear Miriam,
There has been little enough happening this week –

On Thursdays he wrote to Miriam; on Mondays, Tuesdays and Wednesdays he wrote respectively to Jane and Susan and Dorothy. On Fridays he wrote to old friends of his own sex, and he kept Saturdays to clear off arrears of official correspondence, and he hoped on Sundays never to take a pen in hand.

He often thought about using a typewriter and doing four copies at once, but Miriam and Dorothy and Jane

11

and Susan were not fools – he would never have bothered about them in the first place if they were – and they could spot a carbon copy anywhere. There was nothing for it but to write toilsomely to each one by hand, although it did not matter if he repeated the phraseology; not one of those girls knew any of the others, thank God, and if they did, they wouldn't compare notes about him, seeing what a delicate affair each affair was.

Scroggs re-entered the room abruptly. 'Message just arrived, sir,' he said, passing over the decoded note.

It was for Captain D. from the vice-admiral, Alexandria, and was marked 'Priority'. It ran:

MUCH GREEK GOLD AWAITING SHIPMENT MERKA BAY. REMOVE IF POSSIBLE. END.

'Not acknowledged, of course?' said Crowe.

'No, sir,' said Scroggs.

Any acknowledgement would violate standing orders for wireless silence.

'All right, Scroggs. I'll call you when I want you.'

Crowe sat and thought about this new development. 'Much Greek gold.' A thousand pounds? A million pounds? The Greek government gold reserves must amount to a good deal more than a million pounds. If Crete was going to be lost – and it looked very much as if it was going to be – it would be highly desirable to keep that much gold from falling into the hands of the Germans. But it was the 'if possible' that complicated the question. Actually it was a compliment – it gave him discretion. It was for him to decide whether to stake the *Apache* against the gold, but it was the devil of a decision to make. The ordinary naval problem was easy by comparison, for the value of the *Apache* could be easily computed against other standards. It would always be worthwhile, for instance, to risk the *Apache* in exchange for a chance to destroy a light cruiser. But in exchange for gold? When she was built, the *Apache* cost less than half a million sterling, but that was in peacetime. In time of war, destroyers might be considered to be worth their weight in gold – or was that strictly true?

There was the question of the odds too. If he took the *Apache* into Merka Bay tomorrow at dawn and risked the Stukas, what would be the chances of getting her out again? Obviously, if he were quite sure of it, he should try for the gold; and on the other hand, if he were sure that she would be destroyed, it would not be worth making the attempt, not for all the gold in the Americas. The actual odds lay somewhere between the one extreme and the other – two to one against success, say. Was it a profitable gamble to risk the *Apache* on a two-to-one chance, in the hope of gaining an indefinite number of millions?

He had only to raise his voice to summon the staff that a thoughtful government had provided. Three brilliant young officers, all graduates of the Naval Staff College, and the main reason for their presence on board was to advise. Crowe thought about his staff and grinned to himself. They would tell him, solemnly, the very things he had just been thinking out for himself, and, after all that, the ultimate decision would still lie with him alone. There could be no shifting of that responsibility – and Crowe suddenly realised that he did not want to shift it. Responsibility was the air he breathed. He sat making up his mind, while the *Apache* rose and fell gently on the Mediterranean swell and the propellers throbbed steadily; he still held the message in idle fingers, and looked at it with unseeing eyes. When at last he rose, he had reached his decision, and it remained only to communicate it to his staff to tell them that he intended to go into Merka Bay to fetch away some gold, and to look over the chart with them and settle the details.

That was what he did, and the flotilla gunnery officer and the signals officer and the navigating officer listened to him attentively. It was only a matter of a few minutes to decide on everything. Rowles, the navigating officer, measured off the distance on his dividers, while the others

13

asked questions that Crowe could not answer. Crowe had not the least idea how much gold there was in Crete. Nor could he say offhand how much a million sterling in gold should weigh. Nickleby, the gunner, came to a conclusion about that, after a brief glance at his tables of specific gravities and a minute with his slide rule. 'About ten tons, there or thereabouts,' he announced.

'This is troy weight, twelve ounces to the pound, you know,' cautioned Holby, the signals officer.

'Yes, I allowed for that,' said Nickleby triumphantly.

'But what about inflation?' demanded Rowles, looking up from the map. 'I heard you say something about an ounce being worth four pounds – you know what I mean, four sovereigns. But that's a long time ago, when people used to buy gold. Now it's all locked up and it's doubled in value, pretty nearly. So a million would weigh twenty tons.'

'Five tons, you mean, stupid,' said Holby. That started another argument as to whether inflation would increase or diminish the weight of a million sterling.

Crowe listened to them for a moment and then left them to it. There was still a little while left before dinner, and he had to finish that letter. As the *Apache* turned her bows towards Merka Bay, Crowe took up his pen again :

. . . but it is most infernally hot and I suppose it will get hotter as the year grows older. I have thought about you a great deal, of course –

That damned monkey was chattering at him through the scuttle. It was bad enough to have to grind out this weekly letter to Miriam, without having monkeys to irritate one. The monkey was far more in Crowe's thoughts than the Stukas he would be facing at any moment. The Stukas were something to which he had devoted all the consideration the situation demanded; it would do him no good to think about them further. But that monkey

14

would not let Crowe stop thinking about him. Crowe cursed again.

— especially that dinner we had at the Berkeley, when we had to keep back behind the palms so that old Lady Crewkerne shouldn't see us. I wonder what the poor old thing is doing now.

That was half a page, anyway, in Crowe's large handwriting. He had only to finish the page and make some appearance of a wholehearted attempt on the second. He scribbled on steadily, half his mind on the letter and the other half divided between the monkey, the approach of dinner-time, Hammett's attitude and the heat. He was not aware of the way in which somewhere inside him his mental digestion was still at work on the data for the approaching operation. With a sigh of relief he wrote:

Always yours,
George

and added at the foot, for the benefit of the censor:

From Captain George Crowe,

C.B., D.S.O., R.N.

The worst business of the day was over and he could dine with a clear conscience, untroubled until morning.

The dark hours that followed midnight found the *Apache* in Merka Bay. She had glided silently in and had dropped anchor unobserved by anyone, apparently, while all around her in the distance were the signs and thunder of war. Overhead in the darkness had passed droning death, not once or twice but many times, passing by on mysterious and unknown errands. Crowe, on the bridge beside Hammett, had heard the queer bumbling of German bombers, the more incisive note of fighter planes. Out on the distant horizon along the coast they had seen the great flashes of the nightmare battle that was being fought out there, sometimes the pyrotechnic sparkle of anti-aircraft fire, and they had heard the murmur of the firing. Now Nickleby had slipped ashore in the dinghy to make contact with the Greeks.

'He's the devil of a long time, sir,' grumbled Rowles. 'We'll never get away before daylight, at this rate.'

'I never expected to,' said Crowe soothingly. He felt immeasurably older than Rowles as he spoke, immeasurably wiser. Rowles was still young enough to have illusions, to expect everything to go off without delay or friction, something in the manner of a staff exercise on paper. If Rowles was still so incorrigibly optimistic after a year and a half of war, he could not be expected ever to improve in this respect.

'The bombers'll find us, though, sir,' said Rowles. 'Just listen to that one going over !'

'Quite likely,' said Crowe. He had already weighed the possible loss of the *Apache* and her company against the chances of saving the gold, and he had no intention of working through the pros and cons again.

'Here he comes now,' said Hammett suddenly; his quick ear had caught the splash of oars before anyone else.

Nickleby swung himself aboard and groped his way through the utter darkness to the bridge to make his report.

'It's all right,' he said. 'The gold's there. It's in lorries hidden in a gully half a mile away and they've sent for it. The jetty here's usable, thank God. Twelve feet of water at the end – took the soundings myself.'

'Right,' said Crowe. 'Stand by to help Commander Hammett con the ship up to the jetty.'

Merka Bay is a tiny crack in the difficult southern shore of Crete. It is an exposed anchorage giving no more than fifteen feet of water, but it serves a small fleet of fishing craft in peacetime, which explains the existence of the jetty, and from the village there runs an obscure mountain track, winding its way through the mountains of the interior, over which apparently, the lorries with the gold had been brought when the fighting in the island began to take a serious turn. Crowe blessed the fore-thought of the Greeks while Hammett, with infinite care in the utter blackness, edged the *Apache* up the bay to the little pier, the propellers turning ever so gently and the lead going constantly.

They caught the loom of the pier and brought the *Apache* alongside. Two seamen jumped with warps, and as they dropped clove hitches over the bollards, Crowe suddenly realised that they had not had to fumble for the bollards. The utter pitchy blackness had changed into something substantially less; when he looked up, the stars were not so vividly distinct. It was the first faint beginning of dawn.

There was a chattering group on the pierhead – four women and a couple of soldiers in ragged khaki uniforms. They exchanged voluble conversation with the interpreter on the main deck.

'The gold's coming, sir,' reported that individual to Crowe.

'How much of it?'

'Forty-two tons, they say, sir.'

'Metric tons, that'll be,' said Holby to Nickleby. 'How much d'you make that to be?'

'Metric tons are as near as dammit to our tons,' said Nickleby irritably.

'The difference in terms of gold ought to amount to something, though,' persisted Holby, drawing Nickleby deftly with the ease of long practice. 'Let's have a rough estimate, anyway.'

'Millions and millions,' said Nickleby crossly. 'Ten million pounds – twenty million pounds – thirty million – don't ask me.'

'The knight of the slide rule doesn't bother himself about trifles like an odd ten million pounds,' said Holby.

'Shut up!' broke in Rowles. 'Here it comes.'

17

In the grey dawn they could see a long procession of shabby old trucks bumping and lurching over the stony lane down to the jetty. All except one halted at the far end; the first one came creeping towards them along the pier.

An elderly officer scrambled down from the cab and saluted in the direction of the bridge.

'We got the bar gold in the first eight trucks, sir,' he called in the accent of Chicago. 'Coins in the other ones.'

'He sounds just like an American,' said Rowles.

'Returned immigrant, probably,' said Holby. 'Lots of 'em here. Made their little pile and retired to their native island to live like dukes on twopence a week, until this schemozzle started.'

'Poor devils,' said Rowles.

Sub-lieutenant Lord Edward Mortimer was supervising a working party engaged in bringing the gold on board the *Apache*.

'Where do you propose to put the stuff?' said Crowe to Hammett.

'It's heavy enough, God knows,' was the reply. 'It's got to be low and in the centre line. Do you mind if I put it in your day cabin?'

'Not at all. I think that's the best place at the moment.'

Certainly it was heavy; gold is about ten times as heavy as the same bulk of coal.

The seamen who were receiving the naked bars from the Greeks in the lorry were deceived by their smallness, and more than once let them drop as the weight came upon them. A couple of the bars, each a mere foot long and three inches wide and high, made a load a man could only just stagger under. It gave the hurrying seamen a ludicrous appearance, as if they were soldiering on the job, to see them labouring with so much difficulty under such absurdly small loads. The men were grinning and excited at carrying these enormous fortunes.

'Hardly decent to see that gold all naked,' said Rowles.

'Don't see any sign of receipts or bookkeeping,' said Nickleby. 'Old Scroggs'll break a blood vessel.'

'No time for that,' said Holby, glancing up to the sky. The action recalled to them all the danger in which they lay; each of them wondered how long it would be before the Stukas found them out.

The first lorry was unloaded by now, and driven away, its place being taken by the second. An unending stream of gold bars was being carried into the *Apache*. The second lorry was replaced by the third, and the third by the fourth. And then they heard the sound of dread – the high incisive note of a fighting plane. It came from the direction of the sea, but it was not a British plane. Swiftly it came, with the monstrous unnatural speed of its kind, not more than five hundred feet above the water. They could see plainly enough the swastika marking on the tail and the crosses on the wings.

'Open fire,' said Hammett into the voice tube.

Crowe was glad to see that there was no trace of hurry or excitement in his voice.

All through the night the gun crews had been ready for instant action. The long noses of the 4.7's rose with their usual appearance of uncanny intelligence under the direction of Garland at the central control. Then they bellowed out, and along with their bellowing came the raving clamour of the pom-poms and the heavy machine guns. The plane swerved and circled. The .50-calibre gun under the end of the bridge beside Crowe followed it round, its din deafening Crowe. He looked down and noticed the grim concentration on the face of the red-haired seaman at the handles.

But that plane was moving at three hundred and more miles an hour; it had come and gone in the same breath, apparently unhit. It seemed to skim the steep hills that fringed the bay and vanished beyond them.

'It's calling the bombers this very minute,' said Holby, savagely glaring after it. 'How much longer have we got to stay here?'

Crowe heard the remark; naval thought had not changed in this respect at least, that the first idea of a naval officer should be now, as it had been in Nelson's day, to get his precious ship away from the dangerous and inhospitable shore and out to sea, where he could find freedom to manoeuvre, whether it was battle or storm that threatened him.

'That's the last of the bars, sir,' called the English-speaking Greek officer. 'Here's the coin acoming.'

Coins in sacks, coins in leather bags, coins in wooden boxes – sovereigns, louis d'or, double eagles, napoleons, Turkish pounds, twenty-mark pieces, dinars – the gold of every country in the world, drained out of every country in the Balkans, got away by a miracle before the fall of Athens and now being got out of Crete. The bags and sacks were just as deceptively heavy as the bars had been, and the naval ratings grinned and joked as they heaved them into the ship.

The first lorry full of coin had been emptied, and the second was driving on to the jetty when the first bombers arrived. They came from inland, over the hills, and were almost upon the ship, in consequence, before they were sighted. The guns blazed out furiously while each silver shape in turn swept into position, like the figures in some three-dimensional country dance, and then put down their noses and came racing down the air, engines screaming. Crowe had been through this before, and he did not like it. It called for nerve to stand and look death in the eye as it came tearing down at him. He had seen men dive for shelter instinctively and futilely, behind the compass or even the canvas dodger, and he did not blame them in the least. He would do the same himself if he were not so determined that the mind of George Crowe should be as well exercised as his body. To watch like this called for as much effort as to put in a strong finish after a twenty-mile run, and he leaned back against the rail and kept his eyes on the swooping death.

At the last possible second the hurtling plane levelled off and let go its bomb. Crowe saw the ugly black blob detach itself from the silver fabric at the same second as the note of the plane's engine changed from a scream to a snarl. The bomb fell and burst in the shallows a few yards from the *Apache*'s bows and an equal distance from the pier. A colossal geyser of black mud followed along with the terrific roar of the explosion. Mud and water rained down on the *Apache*, drenching everyone on deck, while the little ship leaped frantically in the wave. Crowe heard and felt the forward warp that held her to the jetty snap with the jerk. He could never be quite sure afterwards whether he had seen, or merely imagined, the sea bottom revealed in a wide ring where the force of the explosion swept the water momentarily away. But he certainly noted, as a matter of importance, that bombs dropped in shallows of a few feet did not have nearly the damaging effect of a near miss in deeper water.

The second plane's nose was already down and pointing at them as the *Apache* swung to her single warp – Mortimer was busy replacing the broken one. Crowe forced himself again to look up, and he saw the thing that followed. A shell from one of the forward guns hit the plane straight on the nose; Crowe, almost directly behind the gun, saw – or afterwards thought he had seen – the tiny black streak of not a hundredth of a second's duration, that marked the passage of the shell up to the target. One moment the plane was there, sharp and clear against the pale blue of sky; the next moment there was nothing at all. The huge bomb had exploded in its rack – at a height of two thousand feet the sound of the explosion was negligible, or else Crowe missed it in his excitement. The plane disappeared, and after that the eye became conscious of a wide circular smudge widening against the blue sky, fringed with tiny black fragments making a seemingly leisurely descent downward to the sea. And more than that; the third bomber had been affected by the explosion – the pilot must have been killed or the controls jammed. Crowe saw it wheel across his line of vision, skating through the air like a flipped playing card, the black crosses clearly visible. Nose first, it hit the sea close into the shore, vanished into a smother of foam, and then the tail reappeared, protruding above the surface while the nose remained fixed in the bottom.

It was a moment or two before Crowe was able to realise that the *Apache* was temporarily safe; one bomber had missed and the other two were destroyed. He became conscious that he was leaning back against the rail with a rigidity that was positively painful – his shoulder joints were hurting him. A little sheepishly he made himself relax; he grinned at his staff and took a turn or two along the bridge.

Down on the main deck Mortimer had made fast again. But somehow one of the containers of gold coins had broken in the excitement. The deck was running with gold; the scuppers were awash with sovereigns.

'Leave that as it is for now!' bellowed Hammett, standing shoulder to shoulder with Crowe as he leaned over the rail of the *Apache*. 'Get the rest of the stuff on board!'

Crowe turned and met Hammett's eye. 'It looks to me,' said Crowe, with a jerk of his thumb at the heaped gold on the *Apache*'s deck, 'as if this would be the best time in the world to ask the Admiralty for a rise in pay.'

'Yes,' said Hammett shortly, with so little appreciation of the neatness of the jest that Crowe made a mental note that money was apparently a sacred subject to Hammett and had better not in future be made a target for levity – presumably Hammett had an expensive family at home, or something. But Hammett was looking at him with a stranger expression than even that assumption warranted. Crowe raised his eyebrows questioningly.

'There's mud on your face, sir,' said Hammett. 'Lots of it.'

Crowe suddenly remembered the black torrent that had drenched him when the bomb burst in the shallows. He looked down; his coat and his white trousers were thinly coated with grey mud, and it dawned upon him that his skin was wet inside his clothes. He put his hand to his face

22

and felt the mud upon it; the damp handkerchief that he brought from his pocket came away smeared with the stuff; he must be a comic-looking sight. He tried to wipe his face clean, and found that his day-old beard hindered the process decidedly.

'That's the lot, sir!' called the Greek officer.

'Thank you,' replied Hammett. 'Cast off, Mortimer, if you please.'

Hammett strode hastily back to the engine-room voice tube, and Crowe was left still wiping vainly at the mud. He guessed it had probably got streaky by now. He must be a sight for the gods.

Those idiots on his staff had let him grin at them and walk up and down the bridge without telling him how he looked.

The *Apache* vibrated sharply with one propeller going astern and another forward, and she swung away from the pier.

'Good luck, sir!' called the Greek officer.

'Same to you, and thank you, sir!' shouted Crowe in return.

'The poor devils'll need all the luck that's going if Jerry lays his hands on them,' commented Nickleby. 'Wish you could take 'em with us.'

'No orders for evacuation yet,' said Holby.

The *Apache* had got up speed by now and was heading briskly out to sea, the long v of her wash breaking white upon the beaches. Hammett was as anxious as anyone to get where he had sea room to manoeuvre before the next inevitable attack should come. Soon she was trembling to her full thirty-six knots, and the green steep hills of Crete were beginning to lose their clarity.

'Here they come!' exclaimed Nickleby.

Out of the mountains of Crete they came, three of them once more, tearing after the *Apache* with nearly ten times her speed.

Hammett turned and watched them as the guns began to speak, and Crowe watched Hammett, ready to take

23

over the command the instant he should feel it necessary. But Hammett was steady enough, looking up with puckered eyes, the grey stubble on his cheeks catching the light.

The bombers wasted no time in reconnoitring. Straight through the shell bursts they came, steadied on the *Apache*'s course, and then the leader put down its nose and screamed down in its dive.

'Hard-a-starboard!' said Hammett to the quarter-master.

The *Apache* heeled and groaned under extreme helm applied at full speed, and she swung sharply round. Once a dive bomber commits itself to its dive, it is hard for it to change its course along with its target's. Crowe's mathematical brain plunged into lightning calculations. The bomber started at about fifteen thousand feet or more – call it three miles; three hundred miles an hour. The hundredth of an hour; thirty-six seconds, but that's not allowing for acceleration. Twenty-five seconds would be more like it – say twenty before the ship began to answer her helm. The *Apache* was doing thirty-six knots. In twenty seconds that would be – let's see – almost exactly one fifth of a mile, but that did not mean to say that she would be one fifth of a mile off her course, because she would be following a curved path. A hundred and fifty yards, say, and the bomber would be able to compensate for some of that. A likely miss would be between fifty and a hundred yards.

Crowe's quick brain did its job just in time. The bomber levelled off as it let go its bomb, the thing clearly silhouetted against the sky.

'Midships!' ordered Hammett to the quartermaster. The bomb hit the water and exploded seventy-five yards from the *Apache*'s port quarter, raising a vast fountain of grey water, far higher than the *Apache*'s stumpy mainmast.

'Well done, Hammett!' called Crowe, but softly, so as

not to distract the man as he stood gauging the direction of the second bomber's attack.

The *Apache* was coming out of her heel as she steadied on her new course.

'Hard-a-port!' said Hammett, and she began to snake round in the other direction.

The crescendo scream was repeated, but this time the pilot had tried to out-think the captain of the destroyer. The bomb fell directly in the *Apache*'s wake and not more than forty yards astern. She leaped madly at the blow, flinging everyone on the bridge against the rail. And the pilot, as he tore over the ship, turned loose his machine guns. Crowe heard the bullets flick past him, through all the din of the gunfire.

The *Apache* was coming round so fast that soon she would be crossing her own wake. The third bomber was evidently so confused that he lost his head, and the bomb fell farther away than the first one did. Now all three were heading northward again, pursued vainly for a second or two by the *Apache*'s fire.

So they were safe now. They had taken the gold and had paid nothing for it.

Crowe looked aft to where a sailor began to sweep the remaining gold coins into a little heap with a squeegee, and he wondered whether any destroyer's scuppers had ever before run with gold.

Then he looked forward, and then down at the crew of the .50-calibre gun. It was with a shock that he saw that the red-haired sailor was dead; the limp corpse, capless, lay neglected, face in arms, on the steel plating, while the other two hands were still at work inserting a new belt. He had been thinking that the *Apache* had escaped scot-free, and now he saw that she had paid in blood for that gold. A wave of reaction overtook him. Not all the gold in the world was worth a life. He felt a little sick.

The first-aid detachment had come up now, and were turning the body over. A heavy hand fell to the deck with a thump; Crowe saw the reddish hair on the wrist that he had noticed earlier. And then his sickness passed. Forty-two tons of gold; millions and millions sterling. Hitler was starving for gold. Gold would buy the allegiance of Arab tribesmen or neutral statesmen, might buy from Turkey the chrome that he needed so desperately, or from Spain the alliance for which he thirsted. That gold might have cost England a million other lives. Through his decision England had given one life for the gold. It was a bargain well worth it.

Dawn Attack

Captain George Crowe sat at the head of a crowded table in a cabin which it would be an understatement merely to call crowded. For the first time since his appointment as Captain D. commanding the Twentieth Destroyer Flotilla he had the opportunity of a personal conference with the greater part of his destroyer captains. Safely back in Alexandria from the fighting round Crete, he could look round at the grouped figures. There were one or two grey heads, of men older than himself, whom he had passed in the race for promotion, but mostly they were young, eager faces; men desperately proud of their commands and eagerly awaiting the opportunity for further distinction.

In Crowe's hand was a chart, and copies of it were being studied by his subordinates – a chart with a curious history, as was only to be expected, seeing that it contained all the details of the harbour defences of the Italian port of Crotona. There was nothing romantic about the history of that chart; no beautiful woman spy had inveigled it out of the possession of an Italian officer, but it was the product of some weeks of patient work. Every reconnaissance plane which had flown over Crotona had taken photographs of the place and the approaches to it, and, naturally, in a high proportion of the photographs there had appeared pictures of vessels entering or leaving. Correlating these pictures, the naval staff had been able to map out the areas in which ships appeared and the areas in which ships never appeared, and thus had been able to make out a pretty clear picture of the extent of the minefields guarding the port; moreover, by joining on the map the successive positions of the ships photographed entering and leaving, the fairway between the minefields could be accurately plotted.

The photographs of the town itself, diligently compared one with the other, revealed the places of importance sufficient to merit the attention of the Twentieth Flotilla in the operation which Crowe had in mind. The British navy was hitting back; the Battle Fleet was going into the bombardment of Genoa while the Twentieth Flotilla was to take advantage of the protection it afforded to raid Crotona and clean up that pestilential nest of shallow-draft raiders.

Nickleby, the flotilla gunnery officer and the model of all staff virtues, was explaining the various targets to the destroyer captains.

'I've marked the positions each ship is to assume,' he said. 'Also the various aiming points. The MAS depot is at the base of the white cliff at the east end of the town. *Potawatomi*'ll clean that up. *Shoshone*'ll have the wireless masts in clear view, so she'll be able to deal with those. Now, the oil tanks are below a crest – you can see them marked in square G Nine. *Cheyenne* and *Navaho*, in the stations assigned to them, will be able to hit them. Nine degrees to starboard of the line connecting the church steeple and the factory chimney – that's one of their bearings – and range four two double-o will do the business nicely. *Seminole* –'

Nickleby droned on endlessly, outlining the perfect paper scheme in the stuffy heat of the cabin, while Crowe moved restlessly in his chair and studied the earnest serious faces. He felt suddenly incredibly wise and, by deduction from that, incredibly old. Nickleby seemed to him much like some young man describing to his grandfather the Utopian world that ought to be established. Something ideally enchanting, but which made no allowance for the inconsistencies of human nature or for unexpected contingencies. Operations of war never did go the way they were planned. Not even at Zeebrugge, one of the best-planned operations in history, had the attack been able to proceed mechanically; if it had, he would never have had the opportunity of winning the blue-and-red ribbon which he wore. And, of all operations of war, a surprise at dawn was the trickiest of the lot. When Nickleby brought his beautiful paper scheme to him for his approval, he had permitted himself to smile, and the smile had nettled Nickleby, just the way the grandfather's smile of toleration would nettle the Utopian young man. But he had let him go on with it; it was just as well for his officers to familiarise themselves with the problems and the objectives of this particular operation, and this was as good a way as any other, as long as their minds remained flexible enough to deal with the inevitable emergencies when they arose.

Nickleby had finished his explanations now and everyone was looking to Crowe for further remarks. He fumbled for his pipe to give himself time to arrange in his mind what he was going to say, and he grinned benevolently at those young men as he filled it and lit it, and he punctuated his opening words with puffs of smoke, paying close attention to pressing down the burning tobacco. He could remember his own father making just the same gestures. It was queer being forty-two; when he was by himself he felt just the same as he did when he was twenty, but put him with all these young people who treated him as if he were sixty and for the life of him he could not prevent himself from acting like it. It was partly due to his rank, of course; this enforced senility was the penalty he had to pay for the four gold stripes on his arm.

'Nothing' – puff – 'is sure' – puff – 'in a sea fight beyond all others, but' – puff – 'no captain can do very wrong' – puff – 'if he places his ship alongside that of an enemy' – puff. 'Who wrote that, Rowles?'

'Nelson, sir,' said Rowles promptly, and Crowe found himself feeling like a schoolmaster now, instead of a father.

'It says exactly what I want to say,' said Crowe, 'and

29

better than I can say it for myself. Everyone quite clear on what he has to do? Very good, then, gentlemen, I think that will do.'

There was no need for any claptrap appeal to sentiment, fine phrases or historic utterances. Not with those men.

The summer Mediterranean produced a summer storm that night while the Twentieth Flotilla was making its way towards Crotona, and, as is the way with the summer Mediterranean, it took only a short blow to raise a nasty lumpy sea. Crowe, eating his dinner with his staff, noticed the increased motion immediately. The fiddles were already on the tables to prevent the crockery from sliding clean off, and the tablecloth had already been damped to provide enough friction to keep the things more or less in their places, but these precautions were already insufficient.

Holby hurriedly excused himself and left the cabin – the poor fellow was already as sick as a dog in any kind of sea. Crowe cocked an inquiring eyebrow at Rowles.

'Glass is dropping fast, sir,' said Rowles. 'This is going to be a lot worse before it gets better.'

'It might have let us finish our dinner in peace,' grumbled Crowe, and regretted the speech a moment later. He realised that there was at least one profound difference between himself at forty-two and himself at twenty; dinner was much more important nowadays, and he had lost the lighthearted acceptance of the picnic meals served perforce in a destroyer in a heavy sea.

An eighteen-hundred-ton destroyer making thirty knots in rough water behaves in a way to be expected of a ship of her design. The proportion of her length to her breadth is very like the proportions of a lead pencil, and one has only to float a lead pencil in a bathtub and then agitate the water to form a good idea of the antics a destroyer performs in a storm. The higher a gun is mounted above the water's edge, the more efficiently can it be served, so that a destroyer's guns are mounted just as high as is consistent with stability; and on her deck are mounted four ponder-ous torpedo tubes; and the fire-control system also de-mands the loftiest position possible. So that a destroyer is liable to roll just as far as is consistent with the limits of safety; she differs from the pencil in that the pencil rolls completely over and over, while the destroyer only very nearly does. Crowe thought of the pencil analogy several times while that storm persisted and the *Apache* churned her way doggedly through the short steep Mediterranean waves. The seas breaking over the decks made them practi-cally impassable; first she rolled, and then she cork-screwed, and then she pitched, as the wind steadily backed round. The waves hitting her square in the bows sent continual shudders through her, as though some harsh invisible brake had just been applied, liable to tear the unwary from any careless handhold. The miracle was that the flotilla was able to keep together at all. Crowe blessed the fact that he had learned to sleep in a hammock; he had one slung for him and slept stolidly in it, flung about as madly as though in a swing; lying in a berth under those conditions was as tiring as not going to bed at all.

During the day the wind died down, although the sky still remained a sombre grey, but the storm, in its passage down the Mediterranean ahead of them, still flogged the sea into wicked waves, each one of which sent its cor-responding shudder through the frail fabric of the *Apache*.

They did more than that. The modern art of navigation with its precise instruments and accurate measurements is still not quite efficient in the face of Nature at its wildest. Subtle calculations could tell Rowles just how far every turn of the screw had thrust the *Apache* through the water, and accurate meters, more than human in their unsleep-ing watchfulness, could tell him just how many turns the screws had made. But they could not tell him – nor could any instrument on earth – just how many inches each one of those waves had held her back. The marvellous gyro-compass could tell Rowles just what course the *Apache* was steering, but it could not tell him how far she was drift-

31

ing off to leeward with the force of the wind sideways upon her upper works. Directional wireless could help him to fix his position, but in wartime, with the flotilla maintaining the strictest wireless silence, it was not so easy, especially as the farther the *Apache* proceeded on her course, the more acute became the angle she made with the British stations on land and the greater the possibility of error.

Rowles was a brilliant navigator – in no other way could he have become flotilla navigating officer – but the most brilliant navigator in the world, with a lifetime of experience behind him, could not, in wartime, conduct a flotilla through a prolonged storm and at the end of it be sure within ten miles of where he was. In peacetime, as long as one acknowledged the possibility of that error to oneself and was ready to allow for it, ten miles was unimportant, but in time of war, with a surprise at dawn in contemplation, ten miles might mean the difference between success and failure and between life and death.

They all knew that when they clustered on the bridge together an hour before dawn. Holby was still pale with his seasickness, but Rowles was pale with nervous tension. He was attempting to check back in his mind the elaborate calculations he had employed – a quite impossible feat. Nickleby was nervous, too, thinking of the elaborate allocation of targets which he had made, and wondering if, supposing he found at this moment that he had made some error, there would be a chance of rectifying it. It was a moment like those grim seconds before entering an examination room or going on to the field before an important game. Crowe looked at their tense faces; it was an object lesson to him in human nature that these gallant young men, about to plunge into an enterprise of the utmost physical danger, were so much worried at the thought of making fools of themselves that the thought of sudden death did not occur to them at all. It made him smile momentarily, but he checked himself sternly. At too many gloomy wardroom breakfasts could he remember the hostility aroused by the smiling optimist who comes in beaming.

The light was steadily increasing, and the sea had been moderating all through the night. It was no longer necessary to hold on with both hands to preserve one's foothold on the bridge; there was a hand to spare to hold the glasses to one's eyes in a desperate attempt to catch the earliest possible sight of the still invisible land ahead.

Sub-lieutenant Lord Edward Mortimer, R.N.R., was nervous as well. He knew this bit of coast intimately, and he was standing by, ready for his local knowledge to be called into service. He knew it in peacetime; he had anchored his yacht often in Crotona itself, and many had been the brief cruises he had made from there; he had a store of memories of sun-baked beaches and sunburned bodies stretched on golden sands, of beautiful women in lovely clothes, of exquisite ruins on the grey-green hilltops overlooking the blue sea.

'Is that land?' demanded Holby sharply; perhaps seasickness had, as it often does, sharpened his senses.

They all peered through the greyness; little by little what Holby had first seen took form and solidity.

'That's not Crotona,' said Rowles, and there was heartbreak in his voice.

'Do you recognise it, Mortimer?' demanded Crowe.

'It's not Crotona,' agreed Lord Edward, 'it's – ' Lord Edward ranged back through his memories. It was that Viennese girl – he couldn't remember her name now – away back in those impossibly peaceful years. They had gone picnicking with a couple of mules. A cold chicken and a bottle of wine, and some of that sheep's-milk cheese. He could remember the smell of the *macchia* in the sunshine.

'We're seven miles north,' said Lord Edward, 'eight, perhaps.'

It had been pleasant riding back on that shambling old mule over those eight miles.

'You're sure of that?' said Crowe.

3

'Yes,' said Lord Edward. He was sure, although he could not remember the girl's name.

Crowe's staff looked at one another and at Crowe.

'They'll have sighted us already,' said Holby.

'No chance of surprise,' supplemented Rowles, turning the iron in his own wound.

Crowe said nothing, for his mind was too active for speech.

'We can adopt the other plan,' said Nickleby, 'the one we first thought of and discarded. Stay outside the minefield and fire across the neck of the peninsula.'

'Probably that's the best thing we can do,' agreed Rowles.

'Mortimer's right,' interrupted Holby. 'There's the Greek amphitheatre on that hillside.'

Lord Edward remembered that amphitheatre; he had last seen it by moonlight, and he had not been alone.

'Signal "follow me",' said Crowe to the chief yeoman of signals, and then to Hammett, 'Four points to port, please.'

The Twentieth Flotilla wheeled southward like a flight of gulls.

'We've still got a chance of doing damage,' said Nickleby. 'We can signal the other captains to lay on the targets already assigned to them from the new positions. They'll have the sense to know what we're after, and firing over the peninsula might be fairly effective.'

The staff was ready to extemporise, and to make the best of a bad job, and not to admit failure.

'If we strike at once we can still take advantage of surprise,' said Holby. Running in his mind was a whole series of quotations from Napoleon's sayings which had been drummed into him when he underwent his staff training : 'Strike hard and strike quickly.' 'The moral is to the physical as three to one.' 'Victory will go to the side which suddenly produces an imposing force of guns.'

'We're going in through the minefield,' said Crowe, like a bolt from the clear sky. 'Take us in, Rowles.'

His staff stared at him. It had not crossed their minds

for a moment that, having given the enemy twenty minutes' warning of their approach, Crowe would still continue to act upon the original daring plan. With a tremendous effort Rowles exchanged his astonished expression for one of a proper imperturbability. 'Aye aye, sir,' he said, and turned to give the orders to the quartermaster.

The flotilla moved down the sleeping shore and wheeled again at the entrance to the channel.

The rhythm of the throbbing engines beneath their feet changed as Rowles rang down for reduced speed to enable the *Apache* to take the tricky turns. His nerves were steady enough; Crowe was glad to note that, despite the need for haste, Rowles refused to be rattled into a rash handling of the ship. The flotilla followed behind like beads on a string, winding its way along the channel with invisible death on either hand.

'Make the signal for "Commence firing",' said Crowe, and he glanced at Nickleby, who nodded back in return.

Nickleby would give the word for the signal to come down; most of the signals of the British navy, including this one, become operative at the moment when they are hauled down. Everyone on the bridge stood tense, waiting for the shore to break out into a thunder of gunfire. Still no shot was fired; the town of Crotona grew steadily more and more distinct as they neared it, the individual houses standing out like cubes of sugar scattered over the hillside.

They could see the cathedral now, and the steeple of Saint Eufemia, the wireless masts and the gasworks – all the aiming points which were to direct the flotilla's guns – and still there was no sign of activity on the shore.

Safely through the channel, the second division of the flotilla diverged from the wake of the leading one and deployed for action. The long 4.7's were training round, and as the signal came down they burst into a fury of fire. The nine destroyers carried seventy-two 4.7's, and each one fired a fifty-pound shell every four seconds. Crowe stood on the bridge with the ear-splitting din echoing

35

round him and grimly surveyed the ruin he was causing. He saw first one wireless mast and then the other totter and fall. There was a solid satisfaction in seeing the shells bursting in the clustered mass of MAS – the motor torpedo boats on which the Italians had always prided themselves. The factory chimney swayed over to one side and disappeared in a solid block, like a felled tree, and then over the ridge came the satisfactory sign of volumes of thick black smoke; the mixture of high explosives and incendiaries which *Cheyenne* and *Navaho* had been firing had done their business.

A naval bombardment was a much more satisfactory affair than anything that could be attempted from the air; planes might drop bigger bombs, but not with one-tenth of the accuracy of a naval gun, and with none of the chance of correcting the aim which a gun permitted. The *Apache*'s guns ceased fire for a moment and trained round on a fresh target, and then the cargo ships against the quay began to fly into pieces under the tremendous blows dealt them.

But it was in that interval of silence that Crowe heard the rumble of shells passing overhead. The shore batteries had opened fire at last, but they had never been intended for use against ships within the minefield. The startled Italian gunners either could not or would not depress their guns far enough to hit.

'Make the signal for "Second division discontinue the action",' said Crowe. When he heard the harshness of his own voice – the involuntary harshness – he realised the tenseness to which he had been screwed up, and he wondered vaguely for a moment what his blood pressure was.

But this was no time for mental digressions. The second division was heading back through the minefield, and the first division was following them, with the *Apache* covering the rear.

It was more nervous work going out round the turns of the channel even than coming in, for now they were under the fire of the shore batteries. The silence, now that the *Apache*'s guns had ceased firing, was almost oppressive, but Crowe looked with pride round the ship and saw the anti-aircraft guns' crews motionless at their posts, the lookouts sweeping the skies with their glasses, and Rowles' quiet voice giving orders to the quartermaster. The shells rumbled overhead, and enormous jets of water were springing up from the sea, first on this side of the flotilla and then on that. One shell, as it pitched, called up a tremendous upheaval of water, which rocked the *Apache*, an echoing explosion, and a pillar of black smoke.

'Shell touched off a mine,' said Crowe to Nickleby. 'Interesting, that.'

Extremely interesting, for the mine must have been near the surface for the shell to have exploded it – near enough to the surface to damage a shallow-draft destroyer as well as a deep-draft battleship. Crowe had suspected that possibility.

They were through the labyrinth of mines now and the *Apache*'s pulses were beating quicker as Rowles called for full speed to take them out of danger. The bursting of a shell in their wake close astern told them how the sudden acceleration had saved them once again. And then it happened, the shell that struck right between the aftermost pair of guns and burst there. The wounded *Apache* reeled at the rending crash of the explosion, so that Crowe retained his footing with difficulty.

He walked to the end of the bridge and looked aft, but the funnels were between him and the point where the shell had struck, and there was no obvious damage to be seen; only the first-aid and emergency parties doubling aft, the hoses being unrolled and the trail of heavy black smoke which the *Apache* was now leaving behind her. But the beat of the screws had not changed, so that the ship's motive power was uninjured.

He felt the *Apache* heel as Hammett began zigzagging to throw off the aim of the Italian gunlayers. A whole cluster of jets of water sprang up from the point they had just left – some of the spray even splashed round him on the bridge – and the *Apache* heeled again under full helm on a fresh zigzag; it was nervous work waiting for the next salvo, and the next, and the next, while the reports were coming to the bridge of the damage – the aftermost guns completely out of action, the ammunition hoist wrecked, along with the after fire-control station.

It was the price of victory, and a cheap enough price at that. It was not merely the damage done to the Italians – the blazing oil whose thick smoke was making a wide smudge over the now-distant shore, or the shattered MAS, or the wrecked wireless station. The success of the raid meant that in hundreds of little places up and down their coast the Italians would have to redouble their precautions, mount guns and sow minefields, station troops and maintain a constant guard, everything draining fresh strength from an already exhausted country.

'Thank you, gentlemen,' said Crowe, as his staff turned to him when the last salvo had fallen far astern. They were a good lot of fellows who knew their jobs thoroughly. A little academic, perhaps, but that was a fault on the right side. Perhaps in the end they would master the finer points of their profession and acquire the art of putting themselves in the enemy's position and thinking like him.

At that appalling moment when they had found themselves some ten miles from where they expected to be, they had only thought about the enemy academically. They had not realised that surprise was likely to last for many minutes after the initial shock; that the lofty shore which they perceived had been something they were expecting, whereas a sleepy Italian lookout on land had no expectation at all, when he rubbed his eyes and peered through the dawn, of seeing a British flotilla on the horizon, nor had his officers put themselves in the position of the astonished Italians watching the flotilla steam through the minefield, knowing every turn and twist of the channel. In other words, his staff had yet to develop a sympathetic outlook.

Crowe's thought began to stray. Today it was the turn

for a letter to Susan. A dear girl was Susan; it was a pity he would have to confine himself in his letter to inanities and not be able to give the interesting details of today's work. Susan was of the type that would have appreciated and understood them.

What Crowe did not realise was that it was the same telepathic sympathy, the same instinctive estimate of the other's feelings, which made him a success with women and a success in war at the same time.

Depth Charge!

Captain George Crowe, C.B., D.S.O., R.N., stood on the bridge of H.M.S. *Apache* experiencing his first New York heat wave and looking at the skyline of New York from the Brooklyn Navy Yard. The skyline was amazing, just as amazing as the fact that here he stood on the bridge of a British destroyer which was about to be repaired by the United States Government. Commander Hammett came across and stood beside him.

'It's every bit as good as the pictures, isn't it, Hammett?' said Crowe.

'It's the first scenery I've ever seen that was,' said Hammett.

Side by side they surveyed the landscape. Across the East River was downtown New York, while all round them the United States was preparing a navy for war. The din of automatic riveters echoed in their ears, and only a short way off a colossal crane was swinging a huge naval gun into the ship that was to bear it. The *Apache* had made her first contact with American soil; the British ropes were hitched round American bollards and close astern of her towered the bows of the U.S.S. *Coulterville*, a cruiser. Eight thousand tons she was, brand-new, with her fresh paint in striking contrast to the battered and dingy little British destroyer whose white ensign almost brushed her cutwater. On the destroyer's deck little groups of British seamen stared curiously at this fresh country and this fresh navy.

'Well, we're here,' said Crowe. It was a banal sort of

thing to say, but there had been times when he had thought he would never be able to say it; when the poor battered *Apache* had struggled with Atlantic storms and had fought against raiding cruisers.

It had been a long, long journey, and one in which incessant vigilance had been demanded. Even when they had come beyond the radius of action of the Condors, anti-aircraft lookouts had had to be maintained, lest some surface raider with a catapult plane should be on the high seas; all through the thousands of miles there had been the continual anti-submarine watch.

'Well, our troubles are over for a time, at any rate,' said Hammett.

'Let's hope so,' said Crowe. He remembered the very serious talks which he had given to officers and ratings of the *Apache* on the necessity for their good behaviour in America. They were ambassadors of good relations, and they were expected to behave as such.

At the gangway stood a very elegant gentleman. He was wearing a beautifully pressed white suit and a Panama hat; he carried a pair of yellow gloves, and he bore himself, in the studied lack of hurry of his movements, like a typical Englishman in a hot country. It was this deliberation of movement, combined with the perfection of the cut of his clothes, which gave him the advantage of appearing lean instead of merely lanky, and his straight back and erect carriage belied the whiteness of his moustache and hair. Crowe looked down at this morsel of coolness in the sweltering heat.

'I fancy that means trouble, all the same,' he said.

Crowe was right. The visitor introduced himself as Mr Cockburn-Crossley, from the Embassy.

'I have made arrangements for you to pay your formal call upon the admiral commanding,' explained Mr Cockburn-Crossley. 'Can you be ready in half an hour, Captain?'

The watch that Mr Cockburn-Crossley consulted was

just like Mr Cockburn-Crossley, very slim and very elegant and very polished.

'I can,' said Crowe, conscious of the fleeting glance which Mr Cockburn-Crossley had passed over his slightly grubby whites. It was still hardly more than two hours since he had been in the open Atlantic, with the possibility every second of being torpedoed.

'I will expect you, then, in half an hour, Captain Crowe,' said Mr Cockburn-Crossley.

Ever since the heat of New York struck him, Crowe had been thinking about a cold bath, and he retired gratefully into this one; he had yet to learn that in a heat wave in New York one emerges from one cold bath thinking longingly about the next. He dressed himself carefully in his blues. In wartime the glories of full dress and cocked hat and lightning-conductor trousers were discarded. There was not even a sword on board – what they would do if ever a court-martial became necessary, Crowe could not imagine. The mere effort of dressing made him sweat afresh; the tiny cabin under the naked iron deck in the blazing sun was like a furnace, and yet there seemed to be no relief when he stepped out into the open air.

Exactly coincident with his arrival on deck there was a loud splash from astern, an unusual enough noise to attract his attention. What he saw aft, when he directed his gaze there, shocked him inexpressibly. That infernal monkey whom he had detested throughout the long and arduous campaign was standing there gibbering triumphantly and waving in his paw a small glittering object. Crowe raced up to him, but he arrived there no sooner than did Hammett and a perspiring chief petty officer and a couple of ratings.

'Little beggar,' said the chief petty officer. ' 'E's done it proper this time.'

What the monkey had done was to release one of the depth charges that lay ready on the deck for action against submarines.

'Look at 'im wiv the key in 'is 'and,' said one of the ratings.

' 'E's only done what 'e's seen us do often enough,' said the other.

It was withdrawal of the key that actuated the detonating mechanism of the depth charge; the naval rating whose business it was to release the charge would always produce the key to show that he had not forgotten the most important detail of the operation.

'What are those things set for?' demanded Crowe of Hammett.

'Two hundred feet. It's twenty-seven here; and the safety device won't allow the detonator to operate before thirty feet,' replied Hammett, and then, as another series of thoughts struck him, 'But it's a soft bottom. The thing will go on sinking. And the tide's rising.'

'And not just that,' said Crowe, delving back in his mind to recover the memory of the mechanism of a depth-charge detonator. There was a little hole through which water was admitted; regulating the size of the hole regulated the speed at which the water entered, and that controlled the depth at which the charge, slowly sinking from the surface, eventually exploded. But even if, as it soon would be in the present case, the charge lay at thirty feet, the water would still slowly penetrate, and when the detonator was full it would explode, whatever the depth was.

Crowe looked up at the towering bows of the *Coulterville*; the depth charge was under those bows as well as under the *Apache*'s stern, and when the thing should go off, it would do terrible damage to the American ship as well as to the British ship. He did not expect that the *Coulterville* had any steam up to enable her to move; he doubted if even the *Apache* had now. And the explanations which would have to be made before he could get the *Coulterville* to move from her dangerous berth would consume certainly several minutes. He knew that—if he were captain of a new cruiser and an apparently insane

43

foreign officer came rushing up to him in port and asked him to move, he would ask a good many questions before he decided to consent. And what would happen to Anglo-American relations if the first British destroyer to visit Brooklyn were to signalise her arrival by blowing the bows off a brand-new American cruiser was something he did not like to think about.

The seconds were ticking by, although even now probably not more than ten had elapsed since the splash.

'We'll have to send a diver down,' said Crowe. As he uttered the words he visualised the job that had to be done. If that depth charge were to go off while the diver was in the water, the man would be blown to pieces.

'Jones was killed at Crotona,' said Hammett, 'and we left Higgs at Alex. They were the only two divers we had.'

'I'll go myself,' said Crowe. He knew a momentary relief as he said it; the hardest task a leader can ever have is to order some other man into a danger he does not himself share.

'Let me go, sir,' said Hammett.

'No,' said Crowe. 'I took the course myself once; I'm the best qualified. Get the pump and suit out quick, and have some slings rigged over the stern.'

It was twenty years since he had last worn a diving suit and since he had made the three dives which comprised the sketchy course taken by a fair sprinkling of naval officers. He felt the heavy shoes clank over the steel deck as he made his difficult way to the side of the ship. Through the little glass window he could still see the skyline of New York across the East River. The speed with which the gear had been got out and made ready was a credit to Hammett and his first lieutenant; the intense orderliness of a ship of war – even a poor battered old thing like the *Apache* – was justified by this event. No one could ever know when any piece of equipment would be desperately needed immediately. Who ever would have guessed, when they made fast to the shore, that in ten minutes the diving suit would be called for in such a frantic hurry?

44

The air pump whispered steadily in his ear as he trailed pipe and lines behind him. Everything was satisfactory as far as he could see, except that in this appalling climate the sweat was already running in rivers down him and making him itch in a most unpleasant fashion at the same time as the suit prevented him from scratching. He felt his way down the short ladder and then let himself drop down through the muddy, turbulent water. The light faded rapidly from his glass window as he sank, and it was entirely dark by the time he felt his feet sinking into the soft ooze of the bottom. He felt a momentary distaste as he found himself thigh-deep in the filthy stuff. He took a few difficult steps to his left, and then a few forward, and he felt nothing solid. He knew a brief panic, and he swallowed hard. The swallowing seemed to clear his ears and his brain at the same time. He turned to his right and fumbled forward in the darkness with laboured six-inch strides. Then his heavy boot felt and struck it, jarring against something solid, and as he ascertained its shape with his feet he confirmed his first hope. That barrel-shaped thing could only be a depth charge.

He spoke into the telephone. 'I've got it,' he said. 'Send the slings down.'

'Aye aye, sir,' replied a strained voice in the telephone.

He had to wait a second or two for the slings to come down, long enough to feel a gust of savage irritation at the delay, until he remembered that in the increased air pressure of a diving suit every emotion, whether of anger or exhilaration, was proportionally heightened. Then something rapped against his helmet and his eyes took hold of the reassuring slings. He squatted slowly down on his heels, holding the two loops of rope, for he knew the danger of bending forward while wearing a diving suit – at anything more than a slight inclination from the vertical, the protecting air would bubble out, the water rush in, and at that pressure he would be drowned in a flash. Still squatting, and working in the slime, he prepared to guide the loops of the slings over the ends of the depth charge. He

45

had to keep his head clear and make quite sure that the slings were securely round the thing. The depth charge was not lying horizontal, and he put one loop round the lower end and called through the telephone for a pull to be taken on that sling. He felt the rope tighten and the depth charge lurch in the darkness and settle itself horizontally. That was better. He was able to complete his preparations; this was a plain seamanship job, a matter of ropes and weights, to make sure that the depth charge would hang securely in the slings as it was hoisted. If it came loose and dropped again, he could not answer for the consequences. Well, his education in seamanship had begun thirty years ago. His fumbling hands made their last precautionary exploration, then he stood up with a grunt.

'Hoist away,' he said into the telephone.

There was just enough light down here, despite the thickness of the water, to see a faint black shadow rise upward in front of his window. It was a shadow lifted in more than one sense, and he felt his spirits rise with every passing second. He wanted to sing now; he even felt like dancing in his leaden boots and breastplate, in the glutinous ooze – high atmospheric pressure certainly played strange tricks with one's feelings.

The seconds passed and there was no sign of the depth charge redescending.

'We've got it, sir,' said an eager voice into the telephone. 'You coming up, sir?'

'Yes. Hoist away,' said Crowe.

He realised now how deliciously cool it was down here in thirty feet of water, and he grinned to himself at the thought that the best way to get cool in a New York heat wave was to put on a diving suit and go down to the bottom of the East River.

His lines tightened and he was dragged out of the clinging mud, slowly upwards, while the light brightened before his window, increasing steadily until, blinding like a flash of lightning, the direct sunlight struck in through the glass.

He felt the ladder in his grasp and started to climb to the deck with the assistance of a dozen willing hands. They busied themselves about him, whipping off his helmet, and he stood there blinking; even the humid New York air tasted much more pleasant when it had not previously been forced through an air pump. On the deck beside him lay the great barrel of the depth charge, filthy slime dripping off it on to the deck – that was the sort of stuff he had just been wallowing in. The torpedo gunner was hurriedly detaching the detonator.

'I'd say you 'ad about five seconds to spare, sir,' said the torpedo gunner, squinting with a calculating eye at the amount of water that had entered; 'maybe ten.'

'A miss is as good as a mile,' said Crowe. It was a cliché, but he did not feel capable of producing any original thought at that moment. Behind him the monkey suddenly chattered from his perch on the ruins of the after gunhouse.

'Damn that monkey!' said Crowe.

'That's the last mischief he'll get up to in this ship,' said Hammett.

'I'll wring the little beggar's neck, shall I, sir?' said the torpedo gunner eagerly.

'Oh, let the little devil live,' replied Crowe wearily. It was not easy to condemn even a monkey to death in cold blood.

'Wonder if they've got a zoo here?' said the torpedo gunner. 'P'raps they'd take him.'

'Maybe so,' said Crowe. Then he suddenly remembered his appointment with Mr Cockburn-Crossley. 'Here, get these things off me!'

Even the best clothes that Gieve's can supply look rumpled after being compressed into a diving suit. Crowe went below and shouted for fresh clothes to be got out for him; he took another bath and dressed himself as rapidly as the heat permitted, and with all the care the occasion demanded. Then he slung his gold-peaked cap on to his head and hurried over the brow into the clattering din of the navy yard. Mr Cockburn-Crossley was waiting with every sign of impatience consistent with his customary elegant nonchalance. He was putting his watch back into his pocket as Crowe hurried up.

'You're late, Captain Crowe,' he said. 'It is most unfortunate. I wish you could have been more punctual; punctuality is a virtue anyone can cultivate, and it is most important that you should be punctual at this time when we have Anglo-American relations to consider.'

Crowe looked at Mr Cockburn-Crossley for a second or two before he replied, and he swallowed hard too.

'I'm sorry, sir,' he said. 'I was detained by business in the ship that could not possibly wait.'

He felt there was nothing else he could say to Mr Cockburn-Crossley.

Night Stalk

'There aren't any whales in the Mediterranean,' said Nickleby, the flotilla gunnery officer, in tones of deep satisfaction.

'There are big tunny fish, though, that go in shoals,' said Rowles, the navigating officer.

'What about cold currents?' asked Captain Crowe. This discussion dealt with the sort of technical point the solution of which was the task of those highly trained staff officers specifically assigned to him for the purpose; but he knew enough of the subject to take part in the argument.

'Nothing here worth mentioning, sir,' said Rowles. 'Of course, there may be a casual freak.'

'Wrecks?' said Holby.

'Plenty of those,' admitted Rowles.

The flotilla was creeping through the night, guided by the most minute physical influences imaginable – too minute really for the human imagination to grasp, thought Crowe; the merest echoes of something already beyond human senses. They were trailing a submarine. Somewhere inside H.M.S. *Apache* a skilled rating was sending out sound waves into the sea with an apparatus that had never been thought of before Crowe became captain. It was all very difficult, for these sound waves were not the sort that one could hear; they were too high-pitched for that. Crowe could remember being shown a dog whistle once which blew a note too high for the human ear, but which yet could be heard by a dog. The sounds being sent out through the water were the same kind of noiseless sounds

– what an absurd expression ! – but even higher in pitch.

The principle was that when these radiating waves struck a solid body in the water, a minute proportion of them bounced back and could be picked up in the ship by an apparatus even more novel than the one which sent them out.

The fantastic sensitiveness of the whole affair could lead sometimes to curious results – shoals of pilchards off the Cornish coast had been depth-charged more than once; and the dividing wall between a cold current and a warm current could reflect enough of the waves as well as refracting the rest to produce a positive indication in the receiver, so that the ship might find itself launching an attack upon nothing at all, like a blindfolded fighter assaulting a whiff of cigarette smoke.

It was like some deadly game of blindman's buff, or like two men stalking each other with revolvers in a completely dark room, for the submarine was by no means helpless; as she crept about underwater her own instruments could tell her, roughly, the bearing of her enemy, and when she was pressed too hard she could endeavour to relieve herself of her enemy's attentions by a salvo of torpedoes loosed off in the general direction of the pursuing ship.

The little chartroom was hot with the heat of the Mediterranean summer night and the stuffiness which comes with the inevitable interference with ventilation caused by the complete darkening of the ship. Rowles was bent over a large sheet of squared paper on which, with the aid of protractor and dividers, he was plotting the moves of the deadly game.

'*Cheyenne* signals, "Three-four-O",' came the voice of the chief yeoman of signals down the voice pipe from the bridge.

'Three-forty degrees !' exclaimed Rowles eagerly. 'That gives us a fix.'

Cheyenne was in the second division of destroyers out to port and she was giving the bearing of the unseen submarine as deduced from her instruments. Crowe could picture the transmission of the signal, the tiny flashes of the signalling lamp, screened and hooded, so that only the *Apache*, and no possible enemy, could pick them up. Rowles drew another line on his squared paper and made a cabalistic sign at the end of it. 'Mmm,' he said, 'don't think it can be a cold current. And it seems to have moved, so it's not a wreck. Too many propellers going for the hydrophones to help us out.'

Twenty years ago the hydrophone had been the only instrument which could be used for tracking a submarine; it actually listened to the beat of the submarine's propeller, and all the efforts of all the scientists had not yet succeeded in improving it to the point where it could pick up and follow the sound of a submarine's propeller through the noise of those of a whole flotilla.

The message tube buzzed, and Holby snatched the little brass cylinder from it, took out the message and tossed it across to Rowles, who read it eagerly. He ruled another line on his squared paper; the diagram he was drawing there was beginning to take some kind of shape, for the lines all had a general trend, and the little ringed numbers made a series which, though wavering, still had definition.

'I'd like to alter course, sir, if you please,' said Rowles, and Crowe nodded.

Rowles spoke first into one voice tube and then into another. It was only an alteration of five degrees, but, with the flotilla fanned out on a wide front in pitch-darkness and with signals restricted to the barest minimum, it was not such a simple matter to wheel the line round as might at first be supposed. A moment later Rowles asked for an increase in speed, and the officers sitting in the silent little cabin were conscious for a brief space of a change in the tempo of the throbbing of the propellers; at the end of that time they were accustomed to the new rhythm and the throbbing passed unnoticed again. Then came fresh information, messages from the sonic apparatus below and from other destroyers in the flotilla.

'He's altered course,' said Rowles.

The captain of the hunted submarine was receiving indications as well, and was turning his boat in a desperate effort to get out of the path of his enemies. But submerged as he was he could only creep along at six knots, while the destroyers were charging down on him at twenty-five. If only they could maintain contact with him, his end was certain. Rowles wheeled the flotilla farther round to intercept him.

Another voice tube in the little chartroom squeaked a warning, and Holby answered it.

'Torpedoes fired,' he announced. The hydrophone apparatus had picked up the heavy underwater concussion. The Italian was trying to rid himself of pursuit by launching his torpedoes into the midst of his pursuers. Firing under water and aiming only on the strength of the data supplied him by his sound apparatus, he could not hope for very accurate aim; the deployed destroyers made a wide target, but one with a good many gaps in it.

'One hundred and sixty seconds, I should say,' said Holby, and all eyes turned involuntarily on the stopwatch ticking away on the chartroom table. With torpedoes and destroyers approaching one another at eighty knots, each little jump of the hand brought potential death forty yards nearer. Crowe took his attention from the watch and turned it upon Rowles's diagram. The destroyers were headed straight for the submarine, meeting the torpedoes head-on, therefore. That was the best way to receive a torpedo attack – a destroyer is ten times as long as she is wide, and, consequently, the chances of a blind shot missing were ten times as great. There was nothing to be done except wait.

The messages were still coming in, even during that two and a half minutes.

'Gone to ground,' said Rowles, 'on the bottom. It's his best chance, I suppose.'

Lying absolutely silent and still on the bottom, the submarine would give no indication of its position to the hydrophone listeners and precious little to the sonic apparatus. And the Italian captain had taken this action while there was still plenty of time, while the English still were not absolutely sure of his position, and while there was a chance that the arrival of his torpedoes might distract his enemies, throw them off their course and upset their calculations. If he pinned much hope on this, however, he did not know the grim little group that was sitting round the chartroom table plotting his doom. The stop-watch hand was creeping inexorably round. Suddenly the *Apache* stopped as if she had run into a brick wall, throwing them all across the chartroom, and then she reared and then she plunged, standing almost up on her stern and then crashing down again, with the lights flickering spasmodically, while the memory of a tremendous crash of sound echoed in their ears. Crowe had been flung against the bulkhead and the breath driven from his body; it was pure instinct that carried him out on to the bridge; as his eyes were accustoming themselves to the darkness he could feel the *Apache* heeling and turning sharply. A black ghost of a ship whisked past their stern, missing them by a hairsbreadth — that was *Navaho*, which had been following them. The officers and ratings on the bridge, flung down by the explosion, were only now picking themselves up.

'Hard-a-starboard there !' roared Hammett.

'She won't answer, sir !' came the helmsman's reply. 'Wheel's right over !'

The *Apache* was turning sharply in defiance of her helm.

'Bow's a bit twisted, I should say,' said Crowe, peering forward into the darkness, alongside Hammett : he could feel now that the bows were canted sharply downward as well, but in the utter darkness he could form no estimate at all of the amount of damage. The only thing that was certain was that the *Apache* was not on fire; a destroyer full of oil fuel, hit by a torpedo, can sometimes in a few seconds be changed into a blazing volcano.

'Midships!' said Hammett to the quartermaster, and then busied himself with the engine-room telegraph before explaining to Crowe, 'I thought I'd let her complete the turn, sir.'

'Go astern with the starboard engine as she comes round,' said Crowe, and was promptly annoyed with himself for interfering with Hammett when the latter was doing perfectly well.

There were voices to be heard forward now as the stunned members of the crew picked themselves up and the emergency party reached the seat of the damage. The *Apache* was completing her turn, having lost a good deal of her way.

'Hard-a-starboard!' said Hammett again to the helmsman, and the ship trembled with the vibration of the starboard propeller going astern.

From forward there came a tremendous crackling as rivets sheared; the bows of the ship rose perceptibly, she lost her list and drifted on her original course as Hammett stopped the engines.

'We've broken something off,' said Crowe, and a moment later the reports began to come in from for'ard, confirming his suggestion. The torpedo seemed to have hit almost squarely on the bows of the ship and had blown the first ten feet of the ship round at right angles to the rest. It was that which had forced the ship into the turn and which had now broken off. Number 1 bulkhead was holding, however, and the water which was pouring in was no more than the pumps could deal with adequately.

'Get that bulkhead shored up, Mr Garland,' said Hammett.

'Aye aye, sir,' said a voice from the darkness.

'Go ahead with all the speed that the bulkhead will stand,' said Crowe, before he went back into the chart-room.

His staff was still at the table planning the attack on the submarine; Rowles was a little white, and conscious of a stabbing pain every time he breathed, but it was not

54

till some time later that Crowe knew that his navigating officer had broken a couple of ribs when the explosion flung him against the table.

'We'll stay afloat for some time yet,' announced Crowe, 'and we'll make three or four knots, I hope.'

'Splendid, sir,' said Rowles, addressing himself to his squared paper. 'I didn't want the little beggar to get away.'

It is even harder to pick up the trail of a hostile submarine than it is to dispose of her, once she is detected; nothing must be allowed to interfere with the hunt when it is in full cry. While the emergency party faced sudden death shoring up the bulkhead, another signal winked from the battered flagship to the rest of the flotilla, gathering in for the kill. Out on the bridge again, Crowe looked forward through the darkness. He could not see them, but he knew that his other destroyers were arranging themselves in a neat pattern while the poor old *Apache* was panting up after them.

A fresh signal flashed from the *Apache*'s masthead, and it was answered by a sound like a roll of thunder as the depth charges exploded. Only that signal was necessary; Crowe knew that his well-drilled flotilla was weaving round in the darkness as though taking part in an elaborate dance, and every few seconds a fresh roll of thunder announced the completion of a new figure as they systematically depth-charged every possible spot where a submarine might be lying. The sonic apparatus had given them the submarine's position within half a mile; a depth charge bursting within a hundred yards would do grave damage, and it was the business of the flotilla to see that at least one charge burst within a hundred yards. The *Apache* crept slowly over the sea towards the distant thunder; soon she was pitching and tossing perceptibly as the tremendous ripples of the explosions met her. They continued long after the explosions had ceased.

'We ought to be coming up to them now, sir,' said Hammett, gazing into the darkness.

'What's that?' exclaimed Crowe, pointing suddenly.

It was a ghostly white triangle sticking out above the surface of the sea, thirty feet of it or so.

The words were hardly out of Crowe's mouth when one of the forward guns went off with a crash and a blinding flash. That triangle was the bows of a submarine protruding above the surface as she hung nearly vertically between wind and water, helpless and shattered; but a gun's crew, tense and eager for a target, will fire at the first sight of an enemy, and a submarine, once seen, must always be destroyed beyond all chance of escape and repair. The firing ceased, leaving everyone temporarily helpless in the darkness, but, blink their dazzled eyes as they might, Crowe and Hammett could see nothing of that pale triangle.

'She's gone,' said Hammett.

Crowe sniffed the night air, trying to sort out the various smells which reached his nostrils. 'That's her oil I can smell, isn't it?' he said.

Hammett sniffed as well. 'Must be,' he agreed, 'there was no smell of our own oil before this happened.'

The pungent, bitter smell was unmistakable; as they leaned over the rail at the end of the bridge it rose more penetratingly to their nostrils; they could picture the enormous pool of oil which was spreading round them, invisible in the night. And, as they leaned and looked, a vast bubble burst close alongside the *Apache* as some fresh bulkhead gave way in the rent hull of the submarine sinking down to the bottom, and the enclosed air came bursting upward. They heard the sound and, faint in the darkness, they saw a white fragment whirl on the sea's surface.

'There's a bit of wreckage,' said Crowe to Hammett. 'Better get it for identification.'

Wreckage indeed it was, for it was the dead body of a man. They carried it into the captain's day cabin as the nearest lighted place and laid it on the deck. Water ran from the soiled overalls which it wore, forming a little pool, which washed backwards and forwards with the motion of the ship. The stars of gold on the shoulder straps indicated lieutenant-commander's rank; the distorted face was young for a man of that seniority. The arms were clasped across his breast, and there was what looked like a red stain beneath them. Blood? Crowe stooped closer and then took hold of the cold hands and tried to pry the rigid arms upwards; they were clasping to the lieutenant-commander's breast a flat red book, and it was only with difficulty that they worked it loose, so fierce was the grip the corpse was maintaining upon it.

'Send for Mortimer!' snapped Crowe. 'He speaks Italian!'

Most of the Italian that Lord Edward had spoken had been pretty little sentences asking, 'When can we meet again?' and things like that. But he had a good academic knowledge of the language and it took no more than a glance for him to see the importance of what he was looking at.

'It's his orders, sir,' he said, turning the wet pages with care and peering at the smudged handwriting and the typewritten orders that were clipped to the wet sheets.

'What does all this mean?' demanded Crowe. 'Here a latitude and longitude – I can see that for myself. Translate the Italian.'

'He's three days out from Taranto, sir,' said Mortimer, 'and – by George, sir, this looks like a rendezvous! It is, by jingo! And here's the recognition signal.'

As Mortimer translated the typewritten material Crowe looked back at the dead man lying in the puddle on the deck. He thought of the hunted submarine struggling desperately to throw off pursuit, and the final refuge taken at the bottom of the sea, of the rain of depth charges that had brought her up again, shattered and helpless; there would be the rush to destroy the secret documents, and before that could be effected came the shells from the *Apache*, blowing the shattered hull above and giving the captain his death-blow, even while the invading water whirled him to the surface.

'It's authentic all right,' commented Nickleby, peering over Mortimer's shoulder.

'Yes,' said Crowe; 'let's hear it over again . . . Go on, Mortimer.'

The sunken submarine had an appointment with another, in two days' time, so that the one newly come from port could exchange information with the one returning – there was a day, a time and a position. Above all, there was the underwater recognition signal, the sequence of dots and dashes which, sent out in sound waves through the water, would be picked up by the other vessel as a signal for them both to rise to the surface at dawn to effect the exchange.

'I think somebody ought to keep that appointment,' said Crowe, looking quizzically at his assistants.

'There's a bit of difference in pitch between the sound of our underwater signal and theirs,' demurred Holby.

'Not enough to matter,' said Crowe. 'If they get the signal they're expecting, the right signal, at the right time and place, they won't stop to think about a trifling difference in pitch. Put yourself in their place, man.'

The staff nodded. There was something fascinating and magnetic about their captain's determination to do the enemy all possible harm. But it was their duty to look at all sides of a question.

'What about surface propeller noises?' said Rowles, but Crowe shook his head.

'There won't be any,' he explained. 'We'll send one ship – there's no sense in taking the whole flotilla – and she'll get there early in the dark, so she can drift. Who's got the steadiest nerves?'

'Marion?' suggested Nickleby, and as Crowe looked round at the others they nodded an agreement.

'Right !' said Crowe. 'Get the orders out for him now.'

That was how H.M.S. *Cheyenne*, Lieutenant-Commander Edward Marion, D.S.C., came to detach herself from the Twentieth Flotilla at the end of that day to undertake an independent operation while the rest of the flotilla shepherded the wounded *Apache* back to port. It explains how an Italian submarine happened to rise to the surface close alongside her to find herself, much to her astonishment, swept by a torrent of fire from the waiting guns. The official British communiqué, issued some time later, describing the capture, whole, of an Italian submarine, puzzled most of the people who read it. And yet the explanation is not a very complex one.

Intelligence

Captain George Crowe, C.B., D.S.O., R.N., walked down three short steps into the blinding sunshine that made the big aeroplane's wings seem to waver in reflected light. The heat of the Potomac Valley hit him in the face, a sweltering contrast to the air-cooled comfort of the plane. He was wearing a blue uniform more suitable for the bridge of a destroyer than for the damp heat of Washington, and that was not very surprising, because not a great many hours earlier he had been on the bridge of a destroyer, and most of the intervening hours he had spent in aeroplanes, sitting in miserable discomfort at first, breathing through his oxygen mask in the plane that had brought him across the Atlantic, and then reclining in cushioned ease in the passenger plane that had brought him from his point of landing here.

The United States naval officer who had been sent to meet him had no difficulty in picking him out – the four gold stripes on his sleeves and the ribbons on his chest marked him out, even if his bulk and his purposeful carriage had not done so.

'Captain Crowe?' asked the naval lieutenant.

'Yes.'

'Glad to see you, sir. My name's Harley.'

The two shook hands.

'I have a car waiting, sir,' Harley went on. 'They're expecting you at the Navy Department, if you wouldn't mind coming at once.'

The car swung out of the airport and headed for the

bridge while Crowe blinked round him. It was a good deal of a contrast – two days before he had been with his flotilla, refuelling in a home port; then had come the summons to the Admiralty, a fleeting glimpse of wartime London, and now here he was in the District of Columbia, United States of America, with the chances of sudden death infinitely removed, shops plentifully stocked, motor cars still swarming, and the city of Washington spread out before him.

Crowe stirred a little uneasily. He hoped he had not been brought to this land of plenty unnecessarily; he regretted already having left his flotilla and the eternal hunt after U-boats.

The car stopped and Harley sprang out and held the door open for him. There were guards in naval uniform round the door, revolvers sagging at their thighs; a desk at which they paused for a space.

'No exceptions,' smiled Harley, apologising for the fact that not even the uniform of a British naval captain would let them into the holy of holies for which they were headed. There were two men in the room to which Harley led him.

'Good morning,' said the admiral.

'Good morning, sir,' said Crowe.

'Sorry to hurry you like this,' the admiral said gruffly. 'But it's urgent. Meet Lieutenant Brand.'

Brand was in plain clothes – seedy plainclothes. Crowe puzzled over them. Those clothes were the sort of suit that a middle-class Frenchman, not too well off, and the father of a family, would wear. And Brand's face was marked with weariness and anxiety.

'Brand left Lisbon about the same time you left London,' said the admiral. His eyes twinkled – no, 'twinkled' was too gentle a word – they glittered under thick black eyebrows. No man who looked into those eyes even for a moment would want to be the admiral's enemy. Now he shot a direct glance at Crowe, twisted his thin lips and shot a question.

'Supposing,' he asked, 'you had the chance to give orders to a U-boat captain, what orders would you give?'

Crowe kept his face expressionless. 'That would depend,' he said cautiously, 'on who the U-boat captain was.'

'In this case it is Korvettenkapitän Lothar Wolfgang von und zu Loewenstein.'

Captain Crowe repressed a start. 'I know him,' he said.

'That's why you're here.' The admiral grinned. 'Didn't they tell you in London? You're here because few people on our side of the ocean know Loewenstein better than you.'

Crowe considered. Yes, he decided, the admiral's statement was right. He knew Loewenstein. In the years before 1939, the German had made quite a reputation for himself by his bold handling of his yacht in English regattas – Loewenstein and his helmsman. Burke? Of course not. Bruch – Burch – something like that. Good man, that helmsman.

Crowe had met Loewenstein repeatedly on several formal occasions when the British navy had met detachments of the German navy while visiting. And since 1939 their paths had crossed more than once – Crowe on the surface in his destroyer, and Loewenstein two hundred feet below in his submarine.

'Loewenstein,' the admiral was saying, 'left Bordeaux on the thirteenth – that's four days ago – with orders to operate on the Atlantic Coast. We know he has four other U-boats with him. Five in all.'

The shaggy-browed admiral leaned over the desk. 'And Loewenstein,' he added, 'is out to get the *Queen Anne*.'

Captain Crowe blinked again.

'The *Queen Anne*,' pursued the American admiral ruthlessly, 'that is due to clear very shortly with men for the Middle East and India. Men we can't afford to lose. Not to mention the ship herself.'

'What's the source of your information, sir?' Captain Crowe asked.

'Brand here,' said the admiral, 'also left Bordeaux on the thirteenth.'

That piece of news stiffened Crowe in his chair and he stared more closely at the lieutenant in plain clothes. The news explained a lot – the seedy French suit, the hollow cheeks and the haggard expression. A man who had been acting as a spy in Bordeaux for the last six months would naturally look haggard.

Brand spoke for the first time and his pleasant Texan drawl carried even more than the hint that he had not only been speaking French but thinking in French for a long time.

'This is what I brought from Bordeaux,' he said, taking an untidy bundle of papers from the admiral's desk. 'It's the code the German agents in this country use for communications with the U-boats.'

Crowe took the bundle from his hand and gave it a cursory glance. This was not the time to give it prolonged study, complicated as it was, and half the columns were in German, which he did not understand. The other half were in English, and were composed of a curiously arbitrary sequence of words. Crowe caught sight of 'galvanised iron buckets' and 'canned lobster' and 'ripe avocados'. Farther down the column there were figures instead of words – apparently every value in American money from a cent to five dollars had a German equivalent, and the words 'pounds' and 'dozens' and even the hours of the day could convey certain meanings when put in their proper context.

'With that code,' explained Brand, 'you can give time, courses, latitude and longitude – anything you want.'

Crowe braved a question he half suspected he should not have asked. 'Where did you get this?'

'It's not the original,' interposed the admiral. 'The Nazis don't know we've got this. There's no missing original to give them the tip to change their code.'

'A French girl got it for me,' Brand explained.

There was a silence and then the admiral said, 'Well,

Captain, there's the setup. What have you got to suggest?'

Captain Crowe looked down at the floor and then up at the admiral.

'Of course the *Queen Anne* will be secured by convoy,' he said. 'I know you're not thinking of letting her make her regular transport runs without escort. If Loewenstein is waiting for her with five submarines, her speed won't do her any good. And if the Germans know the course and time out of your ports now, there's no guaranteeing they won't know any change in course or time you might give the *Queen Anne*.'

The admiral made a sudden gesture. 'We can send the *Queen* out with half the fleet,' he said. 'But once we're at – map, please, Lieutenant!'

Young Harley spread a map in front of the admiral. Captain Crowe hunched over it, following the line pointed by the top-striper's finger.

'Once there,' said the admiral, 'we'll have to let the *Queen* go on her own. We can't go past that point without neglecting our coastal duties. And Loewenstein is bound to trail along until the escort leaves. Then he'll hit. Unless he can be drawn off.'

'Yes,' echoed Crowe absently. 'Unless we can draw him off.'

'Can we?' the admiral demanded. 'Or – I'm sorry – that's an unfair question, thrown at you all at once, Captain. Think it over and tomorrow morning at' – he glanced at his wristwatch – 'ten we'll talk it over.'

'It wouldn't break my heart,' said the naval-intelligence agent, Brand, suddenly, 'if something drastic happened to Loewenstein. I've seen some of the pictures he's taken with his little camera from conning towers. Close-ups of drowning men – and one that's the pride of his collection, a woman and a kid off the *Athenia*.'

'Something drastic is going to happen to Loewenstein,' said the admiral. He looked at Crowe, and the captain blinked.

'Right-o,' said Captain Crowe.

He found himself outside the office without clearly realising how he got there. He wanted to walk; he was urgently anxious to walk, partly because long hours in planes had cramped his legs – legs accustomed to miles of deck marching – and partly because he wanted to think – had to think – and he thought best on his feet.

He had to draw Loewenstein off. But what could draw a sub commander off a prize like the *Queen Anne*? To sink the *Queen* would give any U-boat skipper the *Pour le Mérite* with oak leaves or whatever brand of decoration Hitler was giving out now. A man would have to be mad to forsake a prize like that. Mad or – but Loewenstein had been half mad that day he had seized the wheel from his helmsman at that Copenhagen regatta and had tried to ram the boat that had overhauled him and blanketed him, stealing the race at the last moment. That Danish club had disbarred Loewenstein for that. But the helmsman had been exonerated. Good man, that helmsman, Crowe thought. Braucht – it was something that started with a *B*. Broening. Yes, that was it – Broening.

Crowe looked around him, squinted at the sun, tucked his chin in his limp white collar and set off boldly in the direction of the British Embassy. He was remembering all he could about Korvettenkapitän von und zu Loewenstein. He called up the slightly pug nose, the cold blue eyes, the colourless hair slicked back from the forehead – he remembered all these. Then there was the ruthless boldness with which he would jockey for position at the start of a yacht race. He would bear down on another boat, keeping his course while the helmsman – Broening – yelled a warning until the other boat fell off. The protest flags fluttered on many occasions when Loewenstein sailed. And after the races, it always was Loewenstein and some beautiful harpy at their table, alone, except for the miserable helmsman, Broening. Now, Loewenstein was the boldest of all U-boat captains.

Crowe knew his lips were not moving, but his mind was speaking. *Draw Loewenstein off*, it said. *But how? Loe-*

wenstein is a believer in the guns, as shown by his record. He conserves his torpedoes to the last. The ideal method of attack, according to Loewenstein, is to rise to the surface at night, preferably when there is just enough moon, or shore-light glare, to give a good silhouette of the target. He times his rise so that the convoy is almost upon him. Then he uses his guns furiously, pumping shells into every hull he can see; his whole pack of U-boats firing together. Then, before the escort comes up, even before the deck guns of the freighters can go into action, his sub flotilla submerges and scatters on divergent courses that confuse surface listening posts so that the escort destroyers don't know the exact spot over which to make their run. Damned clever – except he thinks the Americans don't know how he works. And I – God help me – have been brought over here to show Loewenstein he guessed wrong. But what is it about Broening that's so important? Why do I keep thinking about him?

It would be eight or nine days before Loewenstein and his pack could be expected off the American coast. In that time the moon would be past its full. Three-quarters, rising about eleven. So that it might be best to –

Crowe forgot the sweat that dripped down his face – everything except the problem at hand. It was something that even in his wide experience he had not encountered before, this opportunity of sending orders to an enemy in the sure and certain knowledge that they would be received and acted upon.

Broening, he told himself. *Last I heard of him was that he'd become a Johnny come lately in the Nazi Party and Von Ribbentrop had sent him to some little Latin American country as a consul. Loewenstein must have loved that. Always hated the man, Loewenstein did, even though he won races for him. Now, despite all Loewenstein's Junker background, it seems that Broening is outstripping him in the race for prestige. I'll wager Loewenstein would like nothing better than to – I believe I have it.*

The shower bath offered him by a friend in need at the

66

Embassy was something for which he would have given a month's pay. He stepped under the cold rain and pranced about solemnly while the healing water washed away the heat and his irritation. A plan to deal with Loewenstein was forming in his mind, and as he cooled down, his spirits rose and he nearly began to sing, until he remembered that he was on the dignified premises of the British Embassy. But he still grew happier and happier until he was struck by a fresh realisation. Then his spirits fell abruptly. He had not written either to Susan or Dorothy this week, thanks to the hours spent travelling from England. And today was nearly over, and tomorrow he would have to write to Miriam – three letters pressing on him, to say nothing of the official report he would have to write. Crowe groaned and stayed under the shower a minute longer than he need have done in order to postpone the evil moment when he would have to come out and face a world in which letters had to be written, and when he did he was cursing himself for a soft-hearted fool for not cutting off the correspondence and saving himself a great deal of trouble.

But outside, the assistant naval attaché welcomed him with a smile.

'Here's Miss Haycraft,' he said. 'I thought you'd like her assistance in writing your report. You needn't worry about her – she knows more secrets than the Admiralty itself.'

Miss Haycraft was a pleasant little fair-haired thing with an unobtrusive air of complete efficiency. She sat down with her notebook in just the right way to start Crowe off pouring out his report of his interview with the admiral and Lieutenant Brand.

Half-way through his discourse, Captain Crowe stopped. 'I wonder if the Embassy has any records on a man named Broening?' he asked. 'Nazi fellow. Believe he was consul or minister or something in a Central American state. I –'

'Yes, Captain,' said Miss Haycraft crisply. 'Herr Broening is in New York, waiting to take passage on the diplomatic-exchange ship, *Frottingholm*.'

'Ah?' asked Crowe. 'And when does the *Frottingholm* sail?'

'It's not definite,' the girl answered. 'There's some trouble getting Berlin to assure safe passage.'

'Umm,' said Captain Crowe.

In another ten minutes the report was done. Crowe looked at Miss Haycraft and felt temptation – not temptation with regard to Miss Haycraft, however; she was not the girl to offer it.

'Was the A. N. A. really speaking the truth when he said you could be trusted with a secret?' he asked.

'Yes,' said Miss Haycraft, and her manner implied that there was no need at all to enlarge on the subject.

'All right then,' said Crowe, taking the plunge. 'Take this letter – Dear Susan : As you will see, I have got hold of a typewriter and I am trying my hand at it. Please forgive me this week for being so impersonal, but I have had a good deal to do. I wish you could guess where I am now; all I can say is I wish you were here with me because –'

The letter to Susan ran off as smoothly as oil; it was even more impressive than the writing of the report. When it was finished, Crowe looked at Miss Haycraft once more. Well, he might as well be hanged for sheep as for lamb.

'I'd like you,' he said, 'to do that letter over three times – no, you might as well make it four. Begin 'em "Dear Susan", "Dear Dorothy", "Dear Miriam" and "Dear Jane". – no, not "Dear Jane". You'd better say "Dearest Jane". Have you got that right?'

'Yes, Captain Crowe,' said Miss Haycraft, and she did not even smile.

This was marvellous; his conscience was clear for a week, and Crowe felt more like singing than ever, but he had to restrain himself. He did not mind letting Miss Haycraft into the secret of his epistolary amours, but singing in front of her was another matter. Perhaps it was the mounting internal pressure arising from the suppression of his desire that led to the rapid evolution in his mind of the plan to discomfit Loewenstein.

All I need, he told himself, *is an old hulk with a loose propeller shaft, a quick job of maritime face-lifting, and some co-operation from the newspaper and wireless Johnnies. I've a feeling the admiral ought to be able to get those things for me.*

'What can I do for you, Mr O'Connor?' asked the manager of the broadcasting station, after he had offered his unknown visitor a chair.

Mr O'Connor displayed a badge held in the palm of his hand and passed an unsealed envelope across the desk to the manager.

'Very glad to do anything I can,' said the head of the broadcasting station, when he read the enclosed letter.

Mr O'Connor produced a couple of typewritten sheets of paper.

'That goes on the air,' he said, 'at eleven o'clock tomorrow morning, at Reitz's usual time.'

The manager looked at the sheets. It was the usual kind of broadcast for which Mr Reitz paid twice a week, advertising the goods for sale in his store – galvanised buckets at sixty-nine cents. Grade A canned peaches at thirty-nine cents, and so on. The turns of phrase, the arrangement of the wording bore the closest possible resemblance to Mr Reitz's usual style.

'I suppose I'll have to do it,' said the station manager. 'Glad to do anything to help, as I said. But what is Reitz going to say when he hears it?'

'He may hear it,' said O'Connor dryly, 'but he won't be in a position to object. He'll be in a safe place, and I don't expect it'll be long before he's in a safer place still.'

'I see,' said the station manager.

There was nothing more to be said on the subject of Mr Reitz's objections; it had all been said in those few words and in the glance of Mr O'Connor's hard eyes.

'All the same,' supplemented the FBI agent, 'I would prefer it if you did not discuss Reitz with anyone else.'

'Of course not,' said the man across the desk. 'And this will go on the air at eleven tomorrow morning.'

'Thank you very much,' said O'Connor, reaching for his hat.

'It will be a clear night, Captain,' said the admiral, coming up to the tiny bridge. 'That's the latest forecast.'

'I wouldn't object to a bit of haze myself, sir,' said Crowe.

'If you were in heaven,' chuckled the admiral, 'I'll bet you'd say your crown didn't fit and your harp was out of tune. But you must admit everything's come off slicker than an eel in a barrel of grease. There's the old *Peter Wilkes*, God bless her leaking hull, all dressed up in a coat of white paint and a big sign, DIPLOMAT, on her side, lighted up like a Coney Island excursion boat, wallowing along ahead of us with that fake second funnel threatening to blow off any minute. And her loose screw is kicking up such a fuss that our listeners are going deaf. And here we are, seven of us, coasting along behind that makeshift *Frottingholm*, blacked out and with our men at battle stations. I only hope your hunch is right, Captain. I'd hate to lose that skeleton crew aboard the *Wilkes*. And I'd hate to have this whole expedition turn out to be a howler.'

'It won't,' said Crowe, with an assurance he did not feel. 'Loewenstein hates Broening – always has. He knows if his former helmsman gets back to Berlin safely, Raeder is due to give him a naval command that would put him over Loewenstein. And Germany wants to break up Pan-American solidarity if she can. What better way than to have a U-boat sink a diplomatic ship and claim it was done by you Americans or we British? Loewenstein thinks he can kill two birds with one stone – getting rid of a personal enemy and staging a *cause célèbre* at the same time. And he won't torpedo that ship. He's been told it's

70

without escort, so he'll surface and shell – and machine-gun the lifeboats later, at his convenience.'

'And the loose screw of the *Wilkes*,' observed the admiral, 'will prevent his listeners from knowing we're in the neighbourhood.'

'Right, sir.'

Crowe turned and looked back over the rigid line following behind him. He felt very happy at the imminent prospect of action. He was about to sing, when he remembered the presence of the admiral beside him. Admirals cramped one's style in a manner especially noticeable to a captain whose rank usually made him monarch of all he surveyed.

'Lord Jeffrey Amherst was a soldier of the King,' sang the admiral, as if he were doing it just to rub in the difference in rank. Then he broke off.

'You've no business here at all, you know.'

'None, sir,' agreed Crowe. 'But I'm not the only one like that on board.'

'Perhaps not,' grinned the admiral.

The sun was down now and the darkness was increasing rapidly. The false-faced *Frottingholm* lurched and staggered in the rising seas, a boldly lighted figure on a darkening seascape. The destroyer which Crowe rode rose and fell to the long Atlantic rollers. The men were at the guns. Down below, there were men with earphones clamped over their heads, trying to pick out the sound of submarine engines beneath the howl of the *Wilkes'* clattering screw. The ship, the whole little squadron, was keyed up, ready to explode into action. Somewhere in the darkness ahead was Loewenstein, rereading, perhaps, the information that had come to him that morning regarding the sailing of the *Frottingholm* with one August Broening aboard, the course and speed and destination of the diplomatic-exchange ship. No one could be quite sure of how Loewenstein would act on that information, but everything that Crowe knew about him led the captain to believe he would attack on the surface, about midnight,

71

with his prey silhouetted against a nearly level moon. And, Crowe hoped, Loewenstein would use his deck guns to carry away the radio antenna first, so that no radio operator could tell the world that a ship carrying Nazi diplomats was being sunk by a German sub.

As always in the navy on active service, action would be preceded by a long and tedious wait. Crowe had learned to wait – years and years of waiting had taught him how.

A bell rang at length, sharply, in the chartroom behind him.

The admiral was inside on the instant, and Crowe overheard a low-voiced dialogue between him and the ensign within. Then the white uniform of the admiral showed up again, ghostly in the dark.

'They're on to something,' said the admiral. 'Can't get a bearing because of the ungodly noise that dressed-up hulk ahead is making. But I think your friend is in the neighbourhood.'

'I hope he is,' said Crowe. He was not merely hardened to waiting; he was hardened to disappointment by now.

'Yes,' said the admiral. Crowe was making himself stand still, and was snobbishly proud of the fact that the admiral did not seem able to do the same. Faint through the darkness Crowe could hear him humming, under his breath, 'Lord Jeffrey Amherst was a soldier of the King'.

Funny thing for an American admiral to be singing, Crowe told himself. Lord Jeffrey Amherst, he had never heard of him.

The bell rang again and yet again, and the information brought each time was more defined. Something on the port bow was moving steadily to intercept the *Wilkes*. And behind them rose the moon.

There was no chance at all of the squadron being surprised, but no one could tell just at which second the shock would come.

Somebody shouted. The gongs sounded. Crowe caught a fleeting glimpse of a long black shape breaching just off

72

the side of the gaily lighted white hulk ahead. Then the guns broke into a roar, each report following the preceding one so closely as to make an almost continuous din. The flashes lit every part of the ship, dazzling the officers on the bridge. The destroyer was turning under full helm; not half a mile away there came a couple of answering flashes, lighting the sullen sea between. Then, as quickly as they had begun, the din and the flashes ceased. The little ship was leaping through the water now, the propeller turning at maximum speed, now that there was no need to deceive listeners at the instruments in the submarines. The squadron was spreading out fanwise in accordance with the drill so painfully learned during preceding years. Someone shouted another order, and the depth charges began to rain into the sea.

Then the destroyers wove together again and the last depth charges searched out the areas that had escaped the teeth of the comb in the first sweep. Reports were coming up from below in a steady stream. The little ship's consorts were sending messages as well.

'We hit two,' said the admiral. 'I saw the bursts.'

Crowe had seen them, too, but submarines have been known to survive direct hits from big shells. But if Loewenstein had been where he might have been expected to be, out watching the effect of his guns and the behaviour of his subordinates, there was every chance that one of the shells had killed him.

'Only negative from down below,' said the admiral.

The instruments probed the ocean depths unhampered, now that the *Wilkes* had cut her engines and was drifting. Reports said there was no trace of the solid bodies the instruments previously had contacted below the surface. Presumably, every submarine, torn open and rent asunder, had already sunk down into the freezing depths.

Crowe took the first full breath he had enjoyed since the admiral had flung his poser at him in the Navy Department office, days before. Now, he knew, the *Queen Anne* could make her run with relative security. Now he knew his hunch had been right: his hunch that Loewenstein would try to murder his helmsman, Broening.

The bell rang and some fresh information came up.

'Some indication of something on the surface. These things are too sensitive, if that's possible,' said the admiral. 'They tell you if a man spits over the side. This'll be wreckage, I guess . . . Listen!' he said suddenly. There was a voice hailing them from the surface. 'A survivor. One of the gun's crew blown into the sea when our shells hit them.'

Survivors sometimes can give even better information than wreckage. They searched carefully in the faint light of the moon to find the man who was hailing them. And when they found him and hauled him on board, Crowe recognised the pug nose and the shape of the head even through the mask of oil. It was Korvettenkapitän Lothar von und zu Loewenstein.

Eagle Squadron

Mr Austin Brewer unlocked his post-office box and ran hastily through his mail. Only the shortest glance was necessary, for there were three of the letters he was looking for, each of them easily identifiable by the big black-lettered labels gummed to them: 'Opened by Examiner No. 4378'. There was no need to read the superscription or look at the foreign stamps; in a year Mr Brewer had grown accustomed to receiving these letters. He did indeed glance at the backs of them, but even that was unnecessary, for he knew the handwriting so well. One letter was from Pilot Officer J. Brewer, 143rd Squadron, RAF, and the other two were from Pilot Officer H. Brewer of the same address. Jim and Harry wrote alternate weeks, and it was three weeks since the last mail had come.

Mr Brewer handled the letters a little longingly, and legally he was quite entitled to open them, for they were addressed to Mr and Mrs Austin Brewer, but he had more regard for Isabelle's feelings than to open them; as soon as he reached home they would open them and read them together. At the thought of that he hurried back to his car.

The way home along the highway and the turning off on to the dirt road to the farm were familiar enough to him to think while he was driving. Three weeks was a long time to wait for letters from one's sons; it was waits like this that rubbed it in about the difficulties caused by the German submarines. Mr Brewer knew well that he was indebted to the fact that his sons had joined the

75

RAF for most of his knowledge of Europe and of the military situation there; otherwise he would never have expended so much diligent care on the reading of the communiqués and the war correspondents' accounts. It was to this reading, far more than to his sons' letters, that he owed his knowledge.

Jim wrote better letters than Harry, but even Jim's letters did not tell a great deal. Mr Brewer knew that the boys could say little about what they were doing, because they were engaged upon such important work that any description of it would involve revealing military secrets. But it was not only that; Mr Brewer was conscious of a more unsatisfactory deficiency – the boys had gradually come to take it for granted that he and Isabelle knew as much about England as they did, and that, of course, was by no means the case. Queer foreign expressions had begun to creep into their letters. Isabelle had comforted him by saying that they were only old-fashioned folk, just like a couple of hens who had hatched out ducklings, and had been surprised by their children's new activities.

Mr Brewer sighed as he stopped the car outside the farm. Isabelle was there, the sun bright on her grey hair, and Mr Brewer climbed out as quickly as his rheumatism permitted.

'There're three letters,' he said, the moment he was in earshot, and he saw the look on her face. The boys' letters might indeed be unsatisfactory, but he knew (and he did not let Isabelle guess that he knew) that she lived only for the arrival of them.

Pilot Officer James Brewer, sitting in the Dispersal Room on standby duty, was conscious of the difficulty of writing a satisfactory letter to his parents. He got as far as 'Dear Mother and Dad'. Then he sat drumming on his teeth with the end of his pen. Most of the things which interested him extremely either would not interest the old folks or could not be told.

The thing that occupied most of his thoughts at the

moment, for instance, was that the squadron had just been equipped with the new Spitfires. Planes that embodied the lessons of a year and a half of life and death warfare, planes on which the safety of millions depended, planes which would affect the history and happiness of children to be born a century from now. Improved Spitfires were just beginning to come off the assembly lines, and the squadron was the first in the air force to be equipped with them.

It was something to be proud of, something he wanted to tell the world about; and he knew it was something that Jerry would be very glad to have positive information about. He would like to tell the old folks how the squadron had been trying the new planes out in formation flying, and how satisfactory the results had been – but there again was something Jerry would give a lot to know. He had been thinking about the new German plane that rumour said was in course of production, the Messerschmitt which would presumably be as great an improvement on the old as the new Spitfire was. The happiness of millions depended on the performance of the new Messerschmitt; he realised that the old folks would be more interested in it because his own life, and Harry's life, might easily depend on it. But that only made a double reason why he could not write about it to them. And seeing that the new Spitfire and the prospect of the new Messerschmitt were all he had thought about for days now, it was terribly hard for him to find suitable topics for this letter he had to write. He looked round the room in a desperate search for inspiration.

Harry was larking with Johnny Coe. Lucky devils, for Harry had written last week's letter and Johnny never wrote letters; apparently he had left behind in his native California not a single friend worth troubling about. Johnny with his red hair and freckles was the most carefree person Jim Brewer had ever known, as well as the most brilliant fighter pilot. Jim did not know whether the two qualities bore any relationship to each other. What mattered was that with Johnny on the tail of his section Brewer knew he had no need for anxiety. The three of them had flown in the same section for months now, and Brewer was solidly conscious that his section displayed perhaps the best teamwork in the squadron, which presumably meant in the world. When he put the deduction aside as petty he wondered, a little grimly, whether that was because he was a member of the RAF or because the English habit of self-deprecation had begun to get a hold on him.

Meanwhile it would be as well if he should display something of the English habit of ploughing steadily on in the face of difficulties. There were two pages to be written after the 'Dear Mother and Dad', Brewer began stolidly with the only opening that occurred to him :

The weather is a lot better now but all the same we haven't been as busy as usual. Mother need not worry about sending us things to eat, as we have plenty, the way I have always told you. Harry is full of beans and sends his love to you both. He has gotten himself a new girl friend, who is a nice piece of work. Marjorie Dalziel is her name, which you don't pronounce the way it is written, like a lot of these British names, but don't you worry about that because she's as nice a girl as you could find anywhere. She is a WAAF officer employed near here.

Brewer's thoughts went off into a technical daydream at that. Mother and Dad would be very interested to hear about the work that Miss Dalziel was doing, but that was quite impossible. He shook himself back into a mental attitude more suitable for the writing of commonplaces, and stared out of the window in search of further inspiration. It was a relief when the telephone bell rang and the sergeant who answered it announced in his usual measured tones, 'Squadron scramble for 15,000 feet, Area P23.'

Brewer dropped his pen on the unfinished letter and raced out of the Dispersal Room along with the others.

78

That madman Harry was still laughing at the top of his voice over his joke with Johnny Coe, but all the rest were silent, reserving their breath as they tore across the field. The crews of four were standing by the machines to see that everything was ready while the roar of the starting engines arose deafeningly on every hand. Brewer hauled on his parachute and flung himself into his machine. Automatically he ran through the routine of making ready for the air, turning on oxygen and radio, fastening the harness and checking the fuel gauges. Then in a flash they were off, flight following flight, the new Spitfires with their unbelievable rate of climb and incredible speed.

England fell away below them. The familiar landscape, over which so many epic battles had been fought, fell into the accustomed pattern, changing steadily with each new increase in height. Brewer knew it so well that he could give a pretty close estimate of the height by the appearances below him. Almost right ahead, the silver line of the Channel appeared, and beyond it the grey line of the Belgian coast; on the one hand were the forty million who fought for freedom and on the other were the two hundred million who only hoped for it. Brewer's reaction to the sight was not nearly so romantic. To see the Belgian coast from P23 meant that they must be nearly at 15,000 feet; sure enough that was what the altimeter said, and the squadron leader was levelling off. The rate of climb of these new Spitfires was unbelievable. Brewer wondered about the new Messerschmitts.

The radio-telephone suddenly started. 'Hullo, Cocoa Leader,' it said. 'Hullo, hullo, Cocoa Leader.'

The voice was a full, rich contralto. Brewer remembered how when he had first been introduced to Section Leader Marjorie Dalziel, WAAF, something familiar about her had puzzled him. It was Harry who had identified her voice as that with which the Operations Room on the ground controlled the movements of the squadron. Harry was on the best of terms with her now; Brewer thought they were in love with each other, for that matter.

This was a war in which men and women fought shoulder to shoulder as nearly as might be, but there could not be many cases where the woman said the actual words that sent the man she loved into action. If only he could tell Mother and Dad about it they would be very interested; also, it would solve for a whole fortnight the recurrent problem of what to say in his letters.

'Hullo, April,' said the squadron leader's voice over the radio-telephone. 'April' was the code name of the Operations Room for today, just as the best-equipped squadron of the Royal Air Force, for today, called itself by the unheroic name of 'Cocoa'. And even so, heroism was not dead, but more alive than ever. 'Hullo, April. Receiving you loud and clear. Any information?'

'Bandits at 15,000 feet over P25,' said April.

Jim Brewer's glances, like those of every fighting man in the air, had been cast in every direction; now they were addressed more especially straight ahead to the eastward, even though – like every man who wished to live – he still continued to pay attention to either side and to the air above him, and particularly to the starboard side, where the sun lay. Then suddenly he switched the radio-telephone over to 'send'.

'Bandits at one o'clock,' he said.

Half a dozen voices said the same thing at almost the same instant. There they were like silver beads on a thread, heading northwards along the Belgian coast, a little to the right of straight ahead – at the one o'clock of the imaginary clock of which the squadron was the centre. Marjorie, down below, could hear her Harry announce the sighting of the enemy.

The squadron leader swung round a trifle to intercept them. Jim Brewer's plane was in his propeller wash for one moment, but the next he had led his section into station again on the new course. Brewer switched on his gunsight, adjusted it, and took the safety catch off the firing test. Oxygen and the sudden excitement of getting into the air had accelerated his heartbeat despite himself, despite the familiarity of all that he had just done; but with these new decisive actions he steadied down, for Brewer had the invaluable attribute of calming in the face of danger. Harry and Johnny Coe, behind him, had the odd habit of growing more hilarious – he could hear them on his radio-telephone shouting nonsense at each other until the squadron leader told them to be quiet.

'Hullo, Cocoa Leader,' came Marjorie's voice over the telephone, 'are you receiving me?'

'Receiving you loud and clear,' said the squadron leader.

'You will continue to patrol P23,' said Marjorie.

They were practically over the edge of the imaginary square already, decided Brewer, looking down at the sea below him. Sure enough, the squadron leader's reaction to the order was an abrupt alteration of course which would keep the squadron within the limits set.

'What in hell?' came the voice of the irrepressible Harry over the telephone.

'Say,' came the voice of Johnny Coe, 'the bandits have altered course too. And it looks like they're the new Messerschmitts.'

The chain of silver beads in the distance had doubled upon itself and then straightened itself out, flying solemnly parallel once more to the Spitfires. Brewer, staring at them as tensely as he could, was inclined to agree with Johnny Coe. They were not 110's, anyway.

'Any further orders, April?' asked the squadron leader. His voice had the lackadaisical ring which is noticeable when the typical Englishman tries to pretend he is not being emotionally stirred.

'No,' said Marjorie. 'Continue to patrol P23.'

Her voice, with the beautiful overtones, was clearly pitched in the same way, to make it as unemotional as possible. She was doing her duty; she was not supposed to be inspiring the men she spoke to. Brewer knew that she knew that the order she had just transmitted would keep the man who was dear to her out of battle for a while longer; but her voice was still unemotional.

The squadron leader turned his command about once more, countermarching them along the very outside limits of the area to which he had been restricted. The Messerschmitts circled away from them and then returned.

'Say,' said Harry, 'what *is* this, anyway. A regatta?'

A whoop and gurgle in Brewer's radio-telephone told him that Jerry was transmitting too; was in fact carrying on an animated conversation – occasionally he could hear scraps of real German speech. Presumably the situation was not clear to the German commander, either; it was strange for each side to be challenging battle like this and yet refusing to take the first step. Brewer's explanation of it to himself was that the higher command on each side was laying some deep trap of which the other side was suspicious.

The notion set him looking about him even more keenly, alert to spot the first sign of the springing of the trap. But there was no sign of anything of the sort in the blue heavens about him nor in the sea below which parted the two immensities of suffering.

There was simply nothing happening at all, and no promise of anything for the future.

'Hullo, April,' said the squadron leader.

'Hullo, Cocoa Leader.'

'We're coming in. Any objections?'

Brewer guessed that the squadron leader did not want Jerry to get even a rough idea of the petrol endurance of the new Spitfire; if they came in now, before there was any question of fuel running short, Jerry would be kept guessing a while longer.

'Wait, Cocoa Leader,' said Marjorie. They could hear her talking to Lemons and to Soda Water – apparently the staff mind that devised code names was running strongly on drinks today – while she arranged for a force to cover the squadron from a surprise attack during the dangerous moments of approaching the ground.

'All right, Cocoa Leader, come on in,' said Marjorie.

Down on the ground the ground crews threw themselves

on the Spitfires, like the crews in the pits working on a racing motorcar. But today there was not much to do; only the oil to check and the refuelling to be carried out. The armourer who attended to the guns, and the rigger and the fitter who examined the plane for damage, stood by with nothing to do. The natural discipline of the RAF prevented them from expressing any disappointment that these marvellous machines had once more ascended and descended without any opportunity to prove their worth. But there was disappointment in the atmosphere, all the same, to be sensed like the effects of a distant thunderstorm. Warfare grows more and more mechanised, and the machines grow more and more marvellous, but the men who man them, and the men who service them, are still just as much human beings as those men who handled the guns at Waterloo or drew bows at Agincourt.

And the squadron leader felt the same when he sat down to write the inevitable report on the doings of the day. He allowed a tiny trace of acidity to creep into his style – the dry official style inculcated at Cranwell – as he told about the enemy aircraft, believed to be the new Messerschmitts, which he had sighted and which had refused battle, but which he could have brought to action if he had not been restrained by the orders transmitted from the Operations Room.

And the wing commander to whom the report was addressed felt much the same when it reached him. He read it carefully, frowned a little at the peevish note which the squadron leader had allowed to creep in, and wrote his endorsement of the facts, if not of the sentiments; his knowledge of the facts was a good deal wider than was that of the squadron leader, because through the Operations Room he had been following a much wider slice of the war that day.

When the report reached the group captain, other papers were put aside immediately so it could be studied without distraction. And after it had been read, the group captain referred back to other reports which had come in, compared them, and made his own deductions from the comparison. His deductions he embodied in a report to the Air Staff; the group captain's view of the war was much wider than the wing commander's; half a dozen operations rooms contributed to its breadth.

And the Air Staff correlated the group captain's report with those of the other group captains, and air commodores made their contribution too, all of them working coolly and rapidly in their effort to gather together all the essentials for presentation before midnight to the air marshal. Along all the various channels, perhaps a hundred thousand facts had come in, and from these the unessentials had to be stripped and the essentials displayed in their proper proportions. But the fruitless encounter between the new Spitfires and the new Messerschmitts had had its place in the final result; the air marshal had already given orders to that effect.

And those wing commanders and group captains and air vice-marshals were links in one chain which ended in the air marshal. The little air raid warden, stubbornly doing his duty in a London back street, was the final link in another chain which ran through the Air Raid Precaution Centre and the Regional Centre and the Ministry of Home Security and the Cabinet Secretariat and the Air Ministry and terminated with the air marshal. And the shelter marshals, the devoted people who knew best what was the condition of the people bombed and homeless, whose reports told how the unnamed millions were standing the strain which none had ever dreamed, in the years before, that they would be able to stand at all, were the final links in another chain – a shelter marshal at one end, and the air marshal at the other.

And there were still other chains; the pitiful reports of bombings and burnings were, essentially, matters of defence, fantastic as the term may seem at first sight. There were reports of offensive matters as well. There were the opinions of the factory inspectors with their information about present production and forecasts of the future. The Ministry of Shipping had its tale to tell about the flow of help from the United States. The Intelligence had reports to make, from facts gathered by patient decoding of German messages, from news sent in by diplomatic officials, from information – one did not dwell on the hangings and shootings which paid for it – acquired by devoted men and women of every nationality from North Cape round to Athens and sent in by routes too obscure for description. The Admiralty came with its contributions regarding the Atlantic bombers and presented its demands for the bombing of German battleships. The War Office had facts to tell and demands to make for air power to assist land forces; even the Foreign Office played its part with its warning of danger developing in new zones and requests for counter-moves.

Along these numerous chains, the facts and the demands poured in to the air marshal; the staff and the Big Five could only sort them. And back again from the air marshal went the decisions – the order for this and the refusal of that. The staff and the Big Five could advise, but it was the air marshal who had to bear the responsibility. He bore the responsibility in the eyes of the public and before the bar of history, but that sat lightly on his shoulders compared with the responsibility of doing his job well before his own conscience.

A million men obeyed his orders; the peace and happiness of thousands of millions unborn, through countless generations to come, depended directly on his decisions. A mistake made now might mean that miserable peasants a hundred years from now would still be slaves; unthinkably it might mean that Britain herself might lapse into slavery. On the other hand, the right plan resolutely carried through, the ingenious device hit upon by good fortune, might shortly spell freedom for millions and the ending of the grim nightmare which encompassed the world.

And despite all this the air marshal was a human being,

like the air vice-marshals and the group captains and the wing commanders and Harry Brewer, pettishly snatching off his helmet. The air marshal was a man of flesh and blood — five feet ten of it — only a little bulkier than in his lean youth. There was some grey in the black hair, and wrinkles round the corners of the prominent grey eyes; the wrinkles told only the same story as the rows of bright ribbon on his chest. The healthy pink of his cheeks made him look younger than he was, and for a man of his age he was remarkably agile and lithe, but he was a human being, for all that. He had his good days, and, sometimes, he had his bad; and as his wife called him Sam, which was not his name, one could guess that somewhere in the past there was a human story in that connection.

Today he looked at the report of the fighter command and narrowed his eyes as he followed up its implications in his mind. Those were the new Messerschmitts, without a doubt, that the 143rd Squadron had seen. The air marshal had a slight personal acquaintance with the squadron leader (although the squadron leader would be amazed to hear that the air marshal remembered it) and knew just how much reliance to place in his judgement; he knew more about the group captains who confirmed what the squadron leader suggested. And there was a message from a Belgian peasant, too, who had seen the new planes on their field, and weeks back there had come a message from a discontented German who worked in a factory, which had given him a good idea of what to expect. The new Messerschmitts were beginning to come off the assembly lines, just as were the new Spitfires which would contend with them.

The air marshal yearned for more knowledge of those Messerschmitts. He wanted to know all about them: their speed and their rate of climb and their fuel endurance and their manoeuvrability; how they behaved in battle and what were their weak spots; especially he wanted to know how they compared with the new Spitfires. Even though the assembly lines were in full swing, even though the machines were coming off them at the rate of over a hundred a week, and some of the arrangements for production, for the manufacture of dyes and the supply of special metals, dated back over a year, there was still the chance that any defect might be made good immediately; and if not, the sooner the business was taken in hand the better. He wanted one of those new Messerschmitts to be gone over carefully by his experts. He would give a good deal of his private fortune – all of it – for the chance to fly one himself.

And he knew, too, that in Germany at that very moment there was someone who was thinking just the same about the new Spitfires. Those Messerschmitts had been displayed over the Belgian coast for the express purpose of challenging battle with the new Spitfires – battle over German territory, where any Messerschmitt that might be brought down would be safe from prying English eyes, and any Spitfire that suffered the same fate could be examined (what was left of it) with painstaking German thoroughness.

No more painstaking than English thoroughness, mused the air marshal. His orders had sent up the new Spitfires to challenge battle over English soil in just the same way, and his orders had kept them from accepting the German challenge. Marjorie Dalziel was one of the people fighting for England whom he did not know at all, but it was through her lips that he had spoken, as if she were some ancient sibyl, the mouthpiece of an Olympic god. It was time the mouthpiece spoke again. The air marshal walked twice up and down his room before he pressed a button on his dictograph and spoke to the air vice-marshal who was his deputy.

'You've seen the report from the 143rd?' asked the air marshal.

'Yes.' The air vice-marshal was a man of few words.

'Tell 'em to try again. You know the conditions?'

'Of course.' The air vice-marshal was really a little hurt at that, until he suddenly guessed that his impish superior was teasing him, in the hope, this time realised, that he would induce him to use two words where one would have done.

'Right. See you later,' said the air marshal, still chuckling as he switched off.

The brain had started an impulse down one of the nerves that radiated from it; at that impulse the mouth would speak and the limb would strike. From the air vice-marshal the impulse travelled to the Air Staff, and from the Air Staff through the group captain, down, down, to the Operations Room and then to the squadron leader, who had the duty of explaining to his pilots what was expected of them.

'You all understand?' said the squadron leader, looking round at his subordinates. 'We want a Messerschmitt, one of those new ones. Dead or alive, but the more alive the better. We've got to bring it down over England. And on no account are we to lose one of our planes over Jerry's country. Anyone can see why.'

They all could, of course; they nodded to show him that they did. Jim Brewer thought what an interesting letter he could write home about all this if it were permissible.

'I've got my own ideas about how it should be done,' said the squadron leader, briefly, 'but I'd like to hear what you blokes have to say.'

He looked round at the young English faces, the Belgian and the two Poles, with the names of their countries sewn on the shoulders of their RAF uniforms; the three Yanks sitting together and so far without any indication of their nationality save for the self-evident one of their intonation.

'If we came down at them out of the sun – ' began Evans, and then stopped as the squadron leader shook his head.

'They've thought of that too,' said the squadron leader. 'They're only up in the mornings. To get between them and the sun means going too far east, right over Belgium.

88

And that's out of bounds for us. We'd only be playing their game for 'em if we did that.'

'If we fought them,' began Dombrowski the Pole, struggling hard with the difficulties of expressing himself in a foreign language, 'just on the edge of the sea, we might have a chance to get one of them, to – to – '

'To cut one of them out, you mean? Force him over this way and then bring him down?'

Dombrowski nodded. But when the squadron leader looked round at the others they shook their heads.

'Too risky,' said the squadron leader. 'We could try it with anyone else, but not with those blokes.'

There was evident agreement among the others who remembered epic battles.

'We want a decoy,' said Jim Brewer.

'Say, listen,' said Johnny Coe simultaneously.

The squadron leader turned to them.

'Jim's got the same idea as me,' said Johnny Coe.

'A decoy's the only way, I think,' said the squadron leader. 'Something that'll get them to forget their orders for a moment.'

'A couple of bombers!' said Brown.

The squadron leader shook his head again.

'There's only one thing that'll make those fellows forget their orders. There's only one temptation big enough. And that's one of our Spitfires.'

'That's right,' said Johnny Coe, 'those guys are pretty cagey.'

The squadron leader looked round the ring of faces again. His mind was already made up, but he was only human, and wasted a second looking round, as a man going to be hanged looks up at the blue sky. The jealous tradition of the RAF is that no task is so dangerous as to call for volunteers. Everyone is prepared to do what he is told and conversely everyone in a position of authority must be prepared to do the telling. He had to select the man who would do the job best; only that. No other consideration could enter into the decision. He wanted the most daring and ingenious flier, the man whose actions would be most likely to deceive Jerry, the man whose quick-calculating mind would be able to draw the proper distinction, in the heat of battle, between daring and folly. Nor was his task of selection made any easier by the wide choice that the enormous talent of the 143rd Squadron offered him. He turned to Harry Brewer.

'You'll be the lame duck,' he said.

'Okay,' said Harry. 'I'll be the lame duck. Or the goat, or what have you. Let's hear some more.'

'I was thinking about trying it this way,' said the squadron leader. He turned to the blackboard behind him with a gesture queerly like that of a schoolmaster lecturing to a class. But there was the difference that in this case the pupils had valuable contributions to make to the debate that followed.

Down in the underground Operations Room things were quiet at present, in this hush before the dawn. There was not a single buzz from the dozens of telephones that brought in the messages from all over the area, from the observers lying back in their armchairs, from the AA batteries, from the aerodromes hidden away in the folds of the earth. The sergeants sat still on their stools; while a battle was in progress they had small enough chance of that. The group captain sat isolated in front of the frosted glass screen, like some minor deity. To Marjorie the simile was a close one, since she knew what thunders he could unleash at a nod of his head. All this elaborate organisation, all these telephones and these flashing lights, all these ministering sergeants and section leaders, were designed to enable the group captain to fight his share of the Battle of England, and to implement in his section the will of the major deity in the underground Central Control Room seventy miles away.

Marjorie saw to it that her radio-telephone mouthpiece was clear. She ran through in her mind the new list of code names so that she could use any one of them without hesitation, and settled herself securely in her chair. Try as she would, she could not keep her heart from pumping furiously when her period of duty began, and she knew by experience that she would be bathed in sweat at the end of her four hours, even though she would not have moved from her chair. The yellow light in the ruled square in the upper right-hand corner of the frosted screen meant that German aircraft were manoeuvring again in the P row, as they had done each morning for days past – the Messerschmitts upon which so much attention was riveted.

Now the group captain gave the order that tensed her still more; she heard the sergeant muttering the words into his mouthpiece; she knew that Harry and the other pilots of the 143rd Fighter Squadron were now running across the field to get their planes into the air. With her mental ear she could hear the roar of the engines revving up; she could hear that sound from her billet when she was off duty, and had heard it so often. A phone bell rang and a red light appeared on the screen. Marjorie switched in.

'Hullo, Embankment Leader. Are you receiving me?'

'Loud and clear,' said the squadron leader's voice. He was 'Embankment' today when yesterday he had been 'Cocoa'. She was 'Card' today instead of 'April'.

'Bandits in P25,' said Marjorie.

Buzzers were sounding in several places in the room now, and the group captain was issuing rapid orders. More lights were appearing on the screen as he played his chess game of death.

'Bandits in P26, at 15,000 feet,' said Marjorie, watching the screen. 'Hullo, Embankment Leader. Somerset at 20,000 in O19.'

'Message received,' said the squadron leader drily.

The group captain growled an order.

'Hullo, Embankment Leader,' said Marjorie, 'carry out operation previously ordered.'

What that meant she had no idea. Now that the battle was really beginning she had steeled herself, and had forced her voice into calm. But this morning duty, with its cold-blooded moves, was far more trying than the whirl and excitement of night duty on the nights when Jerry was raiding, when red, yellow and green lights moved incessantly on the screen, and the white bars of anti-aircraft barrages flashed on and off, and the earth, even down where they were, shook to the fall of bombs and the vibration of artillery.

'Bandits at twelve o'clock.'

That was Harry's voice. It sounded as if he were keyed up a little more than usual. She had thought the same last night when they met for their evening walk, but of course she had asked no questions.

'Bandits at twelve o'clock!'

Half the pilots in the formation must have switched over their RTs to 'end' to get the news off at once; but Harry had been the first. Marjorie watched the red light move across the screen towards where the yellow light of the Messerschmitts wavered on the boundary of P25 and P26.

'Hullo, Card,' said the squadron leader's voice, 'Embankment beginning action.'

Red and yellow lights were alongside each other now. Over her receiver Marjorie could hear confused sounds as the din of a myriad engines and propellers crept in. Twice, loud and sharp, she heard the sound of machine guns as pilots switched over to 'end' with urgent messages to their fellows.

'Watch those wise guys astern!' That was Johnny Coe's voice.

'Bandits below!'

'Keep station, George, damn you.'

It was like hearing football players calling to one another without being able to see the game, but this was a game of life and death. Marjorie had little idea of what was going on. Right at the back of her mind was a recollection of something Harry had told her; that when a Messerschmitt loosed off its cannons it was like the momentary winking of two dull red eyes, visible even in the sunshine of the upper air. Through it all came the staccato orders of the squadron leader; Marjorie's mental fog cleared a trifle and she began to form a hazy picture of a formal battle, fought at long range with nothing risked and no decision likely. Yet that was not like the squadron leader, nor like the 143rd Fighter Squadron.

'All right, Harry.' That was the squadron leader again. 'You ready to do your stuff?'

'All set,' said Harry's voice. 'Say when.'

Marjorie stiffened despite herself.

'Wait for it,' said the squadron leader. 'Jim, keep clear. Let her go, Harry.'

Then there was not a sound for a whole lifetime – for several seconds. Then Harry's voice again.

'All right, Jim.' There was the hint of mirth in Harry's voice that told Marjorie that he was as keyed up as it was possible for him to be. 'Keep off my tail. Give Jerry a chance.'

Then someone else's voice, high-pitched: 'Oh, God, Harry, look out for yourself.'

Through her receiver Marjorie could hear not merely the rattle of machine guns but the bang of cannons as well.

'Line ahead and follow me,' said the squadron leader with the restrained calm that told its own story. 'Don't cut it too fine, Harry.'

'I won't,' said Harry's voice. And then, immediately afterwards, 'These guys behind me seem annoyed about something.'

That was Harry trying to copy the eternal British characteristic of habitual understatement. He was still speaking, 'Sorry, Skipper. You'll have to write off this plane. It was a good –'

The words ended with a bang and a kind of gulp. Marjorie sat shaking in her chair, waiting for the next words but everything was silent for a few moments.

'Hullo, Card,' said the squadron leader, 'operation unsuccessful. Send the rescue launches out.'

Marjorie found her nails were hurting her palms, and she unclenched her hands with difficulty. But, that done, she rallied. She plugged in and sent the message. She passed the news on automatically to the group captain. She realised she had been breaking the first rule of the radio-telephone operator, which is never to grow interested in the messages she sends and hears. A light came on in the screen.

'Hullo, Embankment. Bandits at M26. Are you receiving me?'

'Loud and clear.'

'Somerset at 20,000 in O22.'

The group captain growled again, the way he usually did.

'Hullo, Embankment,' said Marjorie, relaying the order. 'Come on in now.'

'Message received,' said the squadron leader.

The group captain was bringing Somerset and David over into the sector. Marjorie was busy enough transmitting his orders. Even so, she might have found time to think about Harry and wonder whether his voice had stopped because of a hit on his radio-telephone or because – because of something else. She could have wondered whether or not the rescue launches would arrive in time, but she would not allow herself to do so. She finished her four hours of duty still speaking in the calm, disinterested tones which she had so carefully cultivated.

And long before those four hours were over, when the air marshal had hardly returned from his early session of the Big Five, the air vice-marshal addressed him through his dictograph.

'It's a washout this time, sir,' said the air vice-marshal. 'They wouldn't be drawn. Someone over there's being very standoffish about those Messerschmitts. From the squadron leader's report I should say he did all he could. He lost a plane.'

'Where did it fall?' There was sharp anxiety in the air marshal's voice.

'The pilot did the right thing. He crashed it in the sea, five miles off the Foreland.'

'That's all right, then,' said the air marshal.

'The rescue launches picked him up. Slight wound in the leg.'

'All right.' In the grim arithmetic of war a good pilot was worth more than two fighter planes; more than two, but not quite as much as three, in the eyes of a female radio-telephone operator or of an Ohio farmer and his wife.

Nobody can trace the causes of events to their ultimate source, just as it is impossible to trace their effects to their final termination. The air marshal had had a fine fresh egg for breakfast that morning, at a time when fresh eggs were lamentably short in England. It may have been that egg which started it; it may have been some look in the eyes of the air marshal's wife the night before, when he had been able to make enough time to dine with her. It may be foolish to start an investigation into the cause of things as near at hand as that; it might lie much farther back, in some incident in the air marshal's boyhood. But the fresh egg may serve as a basis for discussion; we can at least try to follow up cause and effect from the air marshal's breakfast egg to the receipt of a letter by an Ohio farmer.

The memory of that egg still lingered on the air marshal's palate. He savoured it reminiscently as he listened to the air vice-marshal. It stimulated his robust optimism as well as his imagination. It set his busy mind at work long before the air vice-marshal had finished telling about the rescue launches. He wanted one of the new Messerschmitts more than a miser wants gold, more than a lover longs for his beloved.

'It'll have to be a pinprick raid, then,' said the air marshal.

'Umm,' said the air vice-marshal doubtfully.

'Yes,' said the air marshal with decision. The air vice-marshal had his uses as an *advocatus diaboli*, as a congenital pessimist, as an envisager of difficulties. But this was not the time for him to function; the breakfast egg told the air marshal so definitely. 'The orders must go out to those parachute agents immediately. And the War Office'll have to be told at once; get me the Director of Military Operations. And the Admiralty. Duffy's the man there; I know he's only the deputy assistant, but this'll be his pigeon. No time to lose.'

The air marshal had forgotten the very existence of the breakfast egg as he switched off the dictograph and busied his mind with other details. He had even forgotten the lost Spitfire and the wounded pilot and the recent failure. If it had been a British habit to abandon an enterprise after an initial failure the history of the world would have been different; certainly it would not have been an English-speaking farmer who cultivated that Ohio farm.

Something to the same effect was running through Jim Brewer's mind that evening as he talked to Marjorie in the black night of a Kentish lane, where no single distant light twinkled through the blackout. He had told her of his dash over to the hospital, and how he had found Harry as perky as usual, with four holes in his right leg and none of them serious, according to Harry.

Marjorie had received the news with sober quiet. These people stood up to punishment all right. It was the example of the fortitude of the little citizens in their bombed streets, the stolid public courage in the face of unprecedented disaster, the national doggedness that did not flinch before the prospect of limitless difficulties, which had converted Brewer into something of a crusader. His motives in coming to fight in the RAF would at first have been hard to analyse; they had included a passion for flying, a vague desire for adventure, possibly a yearning for personal distinction. Now he was a crusader; and the British example had so affected him that he could not possibly say so.

He thought of England as a boxer, hard-hit and still fighting back. England was defending herself with the classic straight left of sea power, with the heavy right hand of an air offensive awaiting its chance. The straight left and pretty footwork were giving her a chance to breathe and regain her strength; a boxer of poorer spirit would have fallen before the terrible battering long before, would have lain down and taken the count.

To continue the analogy, at that rate the Air Staff – Brewer had heard the air marshal's name, but never thought of him as a personality – was a pinch of grey matter inside the boxer's skull. And Harry? Harry was nothing more than a fragment of skin which had just been chipped off the boxer's right knuckle. It was the spirit that counted.

It was hard for those unacquainted with England to realise the quiet heroism which kept her still fighting, and it was quite beyond him to describe it in words; that was why he felt so dissatisfied with his letters home.

The silent night was suddenly filled with the sound of aeroplanes.

'Ours,' said Marjorie, after listening for an instant. 'Long-nosed Blenheims. After the invasion ports again.'

'I suppose so,' said Brewer.

He had other ideas, but he was not saying so; not even to Marjorie. Tomorrow's stunt was most strictly secret. Brewer fancied that the Blenheims had another mission besides dropping bombs. So that Jerry would suspect nothing they would probably drop some, though, while the devoted parachutists sank through the darkness, ready for their mission of preparing the attack. The thought started him thinking again about his own part in tomorrow's attack; he and Johnny Coe would be the only members of the 143rd Squadron taking part in it.

He tried to analyse the motives of the squadron leader, who had allotted them the duty. Probably he and Johnny were – he had to shake off a growing English habit of self-deprecation – the best stunt fliers left, now that Harry was wounded. On a mission where five hundred lives were going to be risked, it would be quite mad

7.

to imperil the final success by choosing inferior fliers for the crowning part of it. But there was more to it than that. With Harry wounded, his section was broken up; it would take time to accustom a new pilot to flying with him and Johnny. The most economical course would be to risk the rest of the section, and in the event of failure to train an entirely new section into the ways of the squadron. Better that than to have two or three sections each with a new pilot in it engaged on the sort of duty that fell to the 143rd.

'You don't talk nearly as much as Harry,' said Marjorie. 'Is that because you're the elder brother?'

'I expect so,' agreed Brewer.

The horizon was suddenly torn with a brilliant display of coloured lights. There were white flashes reaching up to the sky, and there were sullen red glares that illuminated the faint mist in the distance. Their ears could just catch the jerky rumble of the anti-aircraft guns that were firing at the English bombers.

'It looks as if they mean business tonight, all right,' said Marjorie. 'Of course they always do.'

The last words were added hastily, and it occurred to Brewer that perhaps Marjorie knew something about tomorrow's stunt. It was very likely that she did, but she certainly would not say a word about it even to him, because for one thing she would not know that he was going to participate in it. To him there was a touch of drama in the situation; that two people as close to each other as he and Marjorie, with a desperate venture before them tomorrow, should not dream of allowing a hint about it to each other, but should confine themselves to discussing trivialities. Air raids, from this point of view, were only trivialities.

'I suppose Jerry will be coming back at us tonight,' said Marjorie. 'I'm going to bed before he does.'

'That sounds like a good idea,' he said, and they began to direct their steps down the lane again.

'I was thinking of going to visit Harry tomorrow evening,' said Marjorie. 'I was hoping that you could come with me.'

'I'd like to, but I've got a date.'

It was not for him to say what kind of date it was; Marjorie could think what she liked.

'All right,' said Marjorie, and she said nothing else. Brewer began to make up his mind that he was going to be fortunate in his sister-in-law.

They had reached the door of her billet now, and Marjorie came to a halt.

'Good night,' said Brewer, taking her hand. 'Don't worry about Harry. He'll be all right.'

He walked on through the village to his quarters, yawning as he did so. The necessity for being up early for patrol had already grained into him the habit of going to bed at an hour which even in Ohio would be deemed early.

Johnny Coe was already in bed and three-quarters asleep in the room they shared. Brewer was careful only to switch on the bed lamp, so as to rouse him as little as possible. Even so, Johnny turned over restlessly, the freckles on his cheek showing in the faint light. Brewer was hardly into his pyjamas before the bed-head light went out abruptly; someone had pulled the master switch and plunged the station into darkness, which meant German bombers in the vicinity.

He got into bed and pulled the covers over himself just as the first roar of a bomb reached his ears, and he composed himself to sleep while the bombers bumbled overhead and the guns opened up. England was in her nightly uproar. Usually at such times he thought of the things he had seen on his visits to London; the burnt-out streets, the craters in the roads, the mothers in the air-raid shelters, the firemen grappling with their tasks, the guns setting the earth ashake. But tonight, despite the current raid, his thoughts were otherwise directed. There was this business of tomorrow to think about. Somewhere there were plans being made and orders being issued; even a pinprick raid called for the most elaborate timing and co-operation between the services. Already there were parachutists seeking out hiding places in Belgium from which they could emerge on the morrow, and he could picture the other arrangements which were being made.

The old analogy of the boxer occurred to him. From the brain the messages were already coursing down an infinity of nerves, tensing the muscles for a feint with the right, ready for a quick blow with the left. The hard-hit boxer was about to hit back; the soldiers and the sailors, the minesweepers and the anti-aircraft, the night fighters and the bombers – if one could only know all that was involved in tomorrow's raid, one would have a complete view of the Battle of Britain. And the ramifications were so numerous that, just like counting sheep, thinking about them one fell asleep. At least Brewer did – to awake clear-headed in the morning and to turn over with the delicious knowledge that there was no early patrol for him this morning. At this moment of waking that fact bulked larger in his mind than the fact that in the evening he would be in deadly peril.

It was when night fell that the little port woke into sudden activity; until then there had been nothing happening that might be guessed at by a stray German reconnaissance machine. But with the coming of darkness it was different. The lackadaisical major in command put out his cigarette and got to his feet.

'Time for us to go,' he said.

Brewer and Johnny Coe rose with him; theirs were the only RAF uniforms among the khaki and the blue. It was only a step from the hotel bar down to the jetty, and they walked slowly, accustoming their eyes to the sudden transition from the lights within to the darkness without. Down the steep street beside them there wound a strange procession. One could not call it ghostly, because it made far more noise than any ghosts could make – the united muffled roar of a thousand motorcycle engines. Yet there was almost nothing to see, for those motorcyclists had been trained to find their way along any road in formation, and yet in darkness, without collision.

'Brewer, you come with me in the *Magpie*. Coe'll go with Captain Brown in the *Thrush*,' said the major.

The shadowy forms of the two armoured barges could now be seen against the jetty. There was a broad gangplank leading into each barge, and over each was pouring a steady river of motorcyclists, up one ramp, down another, and then round and over the flat bottoms of the barges, to come to a halt, tight-packed and yet in order, so that each barge was jammed with silent men sitting on silent machines.

Brewer could guess at the amount of drill and rehearsal necessary to achieve such a result without confusion. The major took him over a narrower gangplank in the bows. Here the darkness was even more complete; Brewer pulled to a standstill just in time to save himself from bumping his nose against a square mass that loomed before him.

'I'll get in first, if you'll excuse me,' said the major. He opened a door in the armoured car and climbed up with Brewer following him.

'Sit down, please,' said the major. 'If you sit still you won't bump yourself.'

Brewer found that out immediately by experience. As he settled himself he became abruptly conscious of something like a machine-gun butt at his shoulder; the roof was only just over his head.

'Damn you, Owen,' snapped the major. 'I've told you before that you're not to eat either onions or oranges when we're going on a stunt.'

Brewer felt the force of the complaint; there were two hard-breathing privates just at his back, and as far as he could tell, one had been eating the one and the other had been eating the other.

'Sorry, sir,' said Owen, 'but we didn't know we was.'

'Something in that, I suppose,' said the major. He bent

his head to peer at the luminous dial of his watch. 'Twenty-fifteen. Ah!'

'Cast off, there,' came a voice from farther forward which Brewer recognised as that of the lieutenant-commander to whom he had been introduced in the hotel.

The barge trembled to the tremendous vibration of the engines, and almost immediately the bows lifted to a wave. They were at sea.

'Escort's outside,' said the major. 'Not that we'll see anything of 'em.'

Sitting in an armoured car in the bowels of an armoured barge on a pitch-dark night, Brewer did not expect to see anything at all.

'We ought to make the run in an hour and twenty-two minutes,' went on the major. 'Bit longer than you're used to.'

'A bit,' said Brewer. His time for crossing the Channel was under four minutes.

'These damn tides are a hellish nuisance when it comes to operation orders timed to the second,' went on the major. 'You can't ever be sure of anything at sea. Fogs and tides and subs. You always have to leave a margin and when you have to observe complete wireless silence the way we have to, 'tisn't always easy.'

'What about mines?' asked Brewer. He would far rather be fighting a Messerschmitt at twenty thousand feet than sitting here in such an unfamiliar – to say nothing of such an oniony – atmosphere.

'We're too shallow for most of 'em,' said the major, 'For contact mines, that is to say. If we came across any of the other kind it'd be just too bad, I expect.'

'I expect so,' said Brewer.

'But you won't be coming back this way, please God,' said the major. 'Not after all the trouble we've been to about you.'

'Let's hope not, anyway,' said Brewer.

'We're more likely to bring it off than not,' said the major. 'It's better than a fifty-fifty chance.'

'Do or die,' said Brewer. 'That's the motto of everyone in this country.'

'It isn't,' said the major with more animation than he had displayed up to now.

'You all think it, if you don't say it.'

'We don't think anything of the sort,' said the major heatedly. 'We just go on and do what there is to do.'

Brewer decided that it was not the best subject for an argument. But he made a mental note of that 'we just go on' phrase. It sounded duller than 'do or die' and meant the same thing.

The barge was rolling and pounding a little in ungainly fashion. Outside could be heard the sound of the waves.

'We can't help rolling like this,' said the major. 'These damn barges are built for quick landings, and they're not very seaworthy in consequence. Still, you can't have everything.'

That was a safe point to agree upon, thought Brewer.

'Hullo, Fantastic,' said Marjorie's voice almost in Brewer's lap making him jump before he realised that it was the radio-telephone speaking. 'Getaway calling.'

'G-E-T-A-W-A-Y,' said the major counting on his fingers. 'Seven minutes to go.' He peered at his watch again. 'Can't answer 'em, of course,' he said. 'Operation's code name's Zacharias tonight. The other thing's useful so as not to tip Jerry off.'

'Hullo, Fantastic,' went on Marjorie's voice. 'Carlo at 15,000.'

'That means five thousand tonight,' explained the major. 'This is where the balloon goes up,' he went on a moment later, looking at his watch without remission.

Brewer heard the roar of bombers overhead as he spoke; directly afterwards he heard the explosions of bombs right ahead, and even the dark interior of the barge was faintly lit by the reflection from the sky of the flashes of bombs and anti-aircraft guns. The bombers were doing their work of distracting the observers on the shore.

'Stand by!' came the loud voice of the lieutenant-commander.

The major's hands were swiftly at work, as he started his engine and ran it up. From behind came a combined roar as the motorcycle engines joined in. The bows of the barge seemed to fall away. A moment later the car was moving forward. It lurched up and then down as it climbed a slight ramp and descended a steep one; water boiled, foaming white, around it for a space, and then Brewer was pressed back into his seat with the tremendous acceleration of the vehicle as they ran up the beach.

'That's the hard part over,' said the major. 'You can never be quite sure what's waiting for you in the shallows.'

The car leaped and bumped about as it tore forwards and upwards. It was climbing the ruined ramp of the sea wall. The major spun the wheel and slipped into high gear. They were on a road so dark, except for the flash of the artillery, that Brewer could see almost nothing, but the major seemed to have no doubts as they raced along. He suddenly stooped a little more over his wheel and pressed the accelerator farther down. There was a crash, a fantastic leap, and they were through whatever it was that had barred the way.

'Umph,' said the major in a tone of satisfaction unusual to him.

They swung right-handed here, and Brewer had hardly recovered his balance when the roadsides suddenly blazed out into flame, the long flashes of the machine guns lighting up everything. Behind him the guns of the car opened up as Owen and his colleagues traversed their guns in a wide circle. But it was only the briefest time that the fight endured; directly afterwards all was dark again and as quiet as it could be in a car going at that speed.

'Hullo, Fantastic,' came Marjorie's voice. 'Getaway calling.'

'Seven minutes again,' said the major. He managed to look at his watch while travelling at that speed.

The air seemed to be full of the sound of planes. Brewer

104

knew the note of the engines – German night fighters. This corner of Belgium was in a pretty turmoil. He wondered if the parachutists dropped the night before had done their work of cutting the telephone wires. A dozen wires selectively cut, or a hundred haphazard, would play old Harry with the German communications for the few minutes that were necessary. Yet it was not of vital importance. The German command could not yet guess the objective of the raid, even if it was possible to circulate the news that one had landed.

On their left front the sky was suddenly lit like day as parachute flares slowly descended.

'That's the place,' said the major.

The incredibly long flashes of the anti-aircraft guns darted up towards the sky, which was dotted with the bursting shells like popcorn in the light of the flares. Then there came the white bursts of the bombs; even at the rate at which he was travelling Brewer could make out that they were being methodically dropped in a ring round the objective. The whole affair was deliriously exciting. The medieval border forays of armoured men jogging along on horses were nowhere near as dramatic as this raid of cars and motorcyclists tearing into a hostile country at sixty miles an hour.

The major spun the wheel to the left so that the car was now heading straight for the volcanic display of the raid on the airfield. They leaped and bumped. Guns spurted fire beside them, and bullets spanged on their armour.

'Give 'em the stop signal behind, Owen,' snapped the major.

The car was drawing to a halt.

'Now the rocket,' said the major, as they stopped. Other cars were stopping beside them; roaring motorcycles were dying away into silence on either flank, and Brewer's dazzled eyes were faintly conscious of shadowy forms running forward under burdens. One or two whistles blew signals. Four sudden pillars of white fire lit up everything ahead, and four stunning explosions shook the earth.

'That fellow's a minute behind schedule,' grumbled the major.

He reached across Brewer and swung open the door for him. 'Here's your guide,' he said. 'Remember Coe'll be a hundred hards to your right. Good luck.'

An enormously burly sergeant loomed up beside Brewer as he dismounted; half a dozen shadowy forms were apparent behind him.

'This way, sir,' said the sergeant.

They scrambled through a ditch and started over the rough ground. Brewer remembered the maps which he had so carefully studied during the day. Ahead of them, to right and to left, there came a sudden burst of firing from machine guns and rifles. It was not until some seconds later that a searchlight suddenly blazed out into the sky, descended slowly and started to sweep the ground. The delay confirmed Brewer in his suspicion that the attack on the airport was completely a surprise; that the Germans guarding the place had no knowledge up to that moment that there was any British force on the mainland. The parachutists of yesterday had done a good job.

A trench mortar banged off with a jet of fire, followed by a burst of flame close beside the base of the searchlight; another and another followed it and the searchlight went out abruptly. Machine guns began to rave, and were answered not only by British machine guns but by the half-dozen trench mortars. The German airport had been fortified (as had been plain from the photographs) against aerial bombardment, and against a possible attack by a small body of disorganised troops; this well-planned attack by trained men who knew exactly what they had to do was a very different story. The trench mortars were steadily knocking out the emplaced German machine guns in the fashion that their lofty trajectory exactly enabled them to do.

They came to a bomb crater; in the darkness it was impossible to guess what the bomb had hit, but it was very plain indeed that it had hit something; there were things that had been men in that crater. Beyond the farther lip they were on the smoother turf of the airfield, hurrying along, stooping close to the ground. Every advantage was with the British – the advantage of surprise over an enemy dazed by a tremendous bombing, the advantage of preparation, the advantage of a known objective. There was no question of capturing the airfield, but the Germans did not know that. All the British wanted was to push a small body of men unobserved inside the ring for a few minutes, and that objective was practically gained before the battle had really begun.

Brewer kept his head clear and called up before his mind the maps that Intelligence had constructed from the photographs. Over here on the right the map had marked a hangar that camouflage had not managed to conceal from the lens. Coe's objective was another on the other side. They crept towards it; Brewer suddenly felt the sergeant's hand grip his arm and hold him back. The sergeant's eyes were more acute in the dark than were his; it was not until then that he saw the shadowy figures grouped about the door of the hangar. But they were not looking into the field; all their attention was taken up by the heavy firing on the other side. The sergeant thrust Brewer back and crept forward with his men to the little group. There was a sudden cry, not very loud; the muffled sound of blows, some gasps and some groans.

'Come on, sir,' said the sergeant.

When Brewer approached, stepping over the things that lay on the ground, the men were already rolling back the doors of the hangar. No one had dreamed of locking hangar doors within a ring fence of machine guns. There was a sudden subdued glow inside the hangar as the sergeant switched on his torch, carefully shaded.

'This what we're after, sir?' said the sergeant.

'Yes. This is it,' said Brewer. He could not help a long sigh escaping him as he made out the outlines of the new Messerschmitt. He clamped down on his nerves with the

107

stolidity that he owed partly to a childhood on an Ohio farm and partly to a long association with the British. 'Roll her out,' he said.

There was a faint breath of wind, more from ahead than across. Over there the machine guns still spoke and the trench mortars still called up their fountains of flame. Brewer climbed in, his torch in his hand; the controls were much the same as in the earlier models he had studied.

'Okay,' he called to the waiting men.

The shattering roar of the engine sounded loud even through the din of the fighting, but Brewer forced himself to sit still and let the engine warm up for as long as he dared take the chance. Then from across the field he suddenly saw the flashes of firing, points of flame stabbing the night. Coe had not been as lucky as he had, and it was time to go. Further delay would be dangerous.

He pushed open the throttle, and the little machine began to hurl itself over the field, bumping madly on the unevennesses of the turf. He pulled back, and the Messerschmitt left the ground, climbing like an express lift. As he banked and turned he saw under his elbow the red stars of the signal from the sergeant's pistol which would call off the attack and send the expedition dashing for the coast again. He himself was over the coast before the stars had burned themselves out. He twirled ineffectively at the unfamiliar radio-telephone, imagining the orders which Marjorie would be issuing from the Operations Room which would allow a Messerschmitt to descend, uninterfered with, on a British field.

Mr Austin Brewer laid down Jim's letter and looked at his wife.

'He doesn't have much to say, does he?' he said, although even then he was careful not to show any bitterness before Isabelle.

'Let's see what Harry has to say,' said Isabelle, with the brightness that was part of her.

They opened the letter and read it between them.

Dear Mom and Dad:
The big news this week is that old Jim has been gonged
for the DFC.

'Gonged?' said Isabelle, with sudden fright in her eyes.
Austin was shaken too, before his memory came to his
rescue. 'The DFC is the Distinguished Flying Cross,' he
said. 'Harry must mean that Jim's been recommended
for it.'

Of course we're all pleased as hell about it in the squad-
ron, although old Jim's just what you'd expect and keeps
his hand over the ribbon half the time.

Maybe Isabelle had a mother's instinct that there was
further important news in the letter, and she skimmed
over the next line or two, until something else held her
attention.

Poor Johnny Coe, the boy from Fresno that I've often
mentioned, is a prisoner and wounded, we don't know how
badly yet.

Isabelle's eyes met her husband's again; she was thinking of some other mother to whom that news would mean
so much more. Then she read on.

They're going to put all us boys from America together
in an Eagle Squadron. Old Jim will be flight-lieutenant.
But your letters will go on finding us, although our address
will be changed.

That meant something to Austin, but nothing to Isabelle, who gave the item of news the attention it merited
from a mother. She turned the page.

And I've been wounded. You mustn't worry about me, because it's not serious, honest it's not. Just a bullet or two in my right leg. I wouldn't let them cable the news to you because I knew you'd worry until my letter came. Honest, it's not bad. I'm going to be married to a nice girl who does war work round here as soon as they let me out, so you can see I'm not bad.

Love from
Harry

'Wounded!' said Isabelle as she finished reading.

'He says it's not bad,' said Austin with a bluffness that he hardly hoped would deceive Isabelle.

'You know what Harry's like,' said Isabelle. She remembered Harry as a little grubby boy. 'He wouldn't say. Not if it was ...'

The tears were beginning to come now. She held the letter in her hand and bowed her head on her husband's shoulder. It is a far cry from an air marshal's breakfast egg to a woman weeping in an Ohio farm, but the chain was complete; so far.

An Egg for the Major

The major commanding the squadron of light tanks was just as uncomfortable as he had been for a number of days. For the officer commanding a light tank there is a seat provided, a sort of steel piano stool, but, in the opinion of the major, it had been designed for men of a physique that has no counterpart on earth. If one sat on it in the normal way, with that part of one which Nature provides for sitting on a stool, one's knees bumped most uncomfortably on the steel wall in front. And contrariwise, if one hitched oneself back and sat on one's thighs, not only was the circulation interfered with to an extent which led to cramps but also the back of one's head was sore with being bumped against the wall of the turret behind. Especially when the tank was rolling over the desert, lurching and bumping from ridge to ridge; on a road one could look after oneself, but it was weeks and weeks since the major had set eyes on a road.

He left off thinking about the sort of shape a man should be who has to pass his days in a light tank, and gave the order for the tank to stop. He climbed out through the steel door with his compass to take a fresh bearing. Out in the desert here an army had to navigate like a ship at sea, with the additional difficulty that inside the steel walls, with the spark coils to complicate matters, a compass was no use at all. The only thing to do was to get out of the tank, carry one's compass well away from its influence, and look over the featureless landscape and mark some patch of scrub, some minor rise in the ground, on which

111

one could direct one's course. He walked stiffly away from the tank, laid the compass level, and stared forward. This was perhaps the five-hundredth time he had done this, and he had learned by long experience the difficulties to be anticipated. There was never anything satisfactory directly ahead on which he could direct his course. There would be fine landmarks out to the right or left where they were no use to him, but nothing straight ahead. He would have to be content with some second best, the edge of that yellow patch on the brown, and he knew very well that it would appear quite different when he got back into the tank again. Furthermore, it would appear more different still when they had travelled a very little way towards it – there had been times long ago, when the desert was new to him, when he had found at a halt that he was more than ninety degrees off his course. He was far more experienced now; five months of desultory warfare and now this last tremendous march across the desert had accustomed him to the difficulties.

Experience taught him to empty his mind of the hundreds of previous landscapes which he had memorised, to concentrate on this one, to note that yellow patch whose edge would be his guiding mark for the next ten miles, and to look back and absorb the appearance of the country in that direction as well. Then he went back to the tank, decided against the piano stool, slammed the door shut, and climbed up on to the roof before giving the word to start. On the roof he could lie on the unyielding steel to the detriment of hip and elbow, anchoring himself into position by locking his toe round the muzzle of the machine gun below him. After a while his leg would go to sleep at about the same time that his hip could bear it no longer; then he would have to change over; three changes – two turns with each foot and hip – would be as much as he could stand, and then it would be time to take a fresh bearing and go back to the piano stool and the other problem of which part to sit on.

He lounged on the steel roof while the tank pitched

112

and rolled under him; it was as well to keep that foot firmly locked below the gun muzzle to save himself from being pitched off. It had happened to him sometimes; everything had happened to him at one time or another. The wind today was from ahead, which was a mercy; a gentle following wind meant that the dust of their progress kept pace with them and suffocated him. He looked away to the left and the right, and he could see a long line of great plumes of dust keeping pace with him as the other tanks in the squadron ploughed their way across the desert. The major was an unimaginative man, but that spectacle never failed to move him. That long line of dust plumes sweeping across the desert had menace and sinister beauty about it. They were like high yellow clouds, and at the base of each a little dot, a nucleus, as it were, sometimes concealed from view by the inequalities of the ground, and every cloud indicated the presence of one of the tanks of his squadron. There were other clouds behind, when the major turned his gaze that way; they showed where the stragglers were trying to regain their places in the line after some necessary halt. The ones farthest back were the ones who had had track trouble or engine trouble. There could be no waiting for them, not in the face of the orders which the wireless brought in, insisting on the utmost speed in this dash across the desert.

Already in the major's mind that total of days already consumed in the march was a little vague. If he set his mind to it, he could have worked it out, but he felt as if he had done nothing all his life except lead this squadron across the desert. Something enormous and of vital importance was happening to the north, he knew – Sidi Barrani and Tobruk had fallen, but his command had been plucked out of that attack and sent off on this wide flanking sweep, and were already a little in the dark about the situation. These Italian maps were of no use at all. They showed things which simply did not exist – he could swear to that from bitter experience – and, in consequence, the major did not know within twenty miles where he was. But somewhere ahead of him there was the sea, across the great hump of Northern Africa which he was traversing, and beside the sea ran the great road which Mussolini had built, and he knew he had only to arrive on that road to start making things unpleasant for the Italians. What the situation would be when he did arrive he could not imagine in the least, but the major had absorbed the philosophy of the desert, and left that problem to be solved when it arose, wasting no mental effort on hypothetical cases which probably would have no resemblance to the reality he would encounter sooner or later.

The squadron was moving on a wide front, impressive on account of the distant plumes of dust, but even so, the width of the front was nothing compared with the immensity of the desert. They had marched five hundred miles so far, and a thousand miles to the south of them the desert extended as far as the plains of the Sudan. Sometimes the major would allow his imagination to think about these distances, but more often he thought about eggs. Tinned beef and biscuits, day after day, for more days than he could count, had had their effect. Nearly every idle thought that passed through his mind was busy with food. Sometimes he thought about kippers and haddock, sometimes about the green vegetables he had refused to eat as a little boy, but mostly he thought about eggs – boiled eggs, fried eggs, scrambled eggs – mostly boiled eggs. The lucky devils who were doing the fighting in the north were in among the villages now which Mussolini had peopled with so much effort; they would have a hen or two for certain, and a hen meant an egg. A boiled egg. For a day or two, eggs had formed a staple topic of conversation when he squatted at mealtimes with the gunner and the driver, until the major had detected a certain forebearing weariness mingled with the politeness with which his crew had received his remarks about eggs. Then he had left off talking about them; in this new kind of war, majors had to be careful not to become old bores in the eyes of the privates with whom they lived. But not being able to talk about them made him think about them all the more. The major swallowed hard in the choking dust.

The sun was now right ahead of him, and low towards the horizon; the sky around it was already taking up the colours of the desert sunset, and the brassy blue overhead was miraculously blending into red and orange. To the major that only meant that the day's march was drawing to a close. Sunsets came every day, and eggs came only once a year, seemingly.

When darkness came, they halted; each tank where it happened to find itself, save for the outposts pushed forward in case the Italians should, incredibly, be somewhere near and should have the hardihood to attempt operations in the dark. The driver and the gunner came crawling out of the tank, dizzy with petrol fumes and stiff with fatigue, still a little deaf with the insensate din which had assailed their ears for the whole day. The most immediate duty was to service the tank and have it all ready for prolonged action again, but before they did that they washed their mouths round with a little of the precious water taken from the can which had ridden with them in the tank all day. It was at blood heat, and it tasted of the inside of a tank — indescribable, that is to say. But it was precious, all the same. There was always the possibility that their ration of water would not come up from the rear; and if it did, there was also the chance that there had been so much loss in the radiators during the day that no water could be spared for the men.

Once, long back, there had been a heavenly time when the day's ration had been a gallon a head a day. That had been marvellous, for a man could do simply anything with a gallon a day; he could shave, wash his face, sometimes even spare a little to wash off the irritating dust from his body. But the ration, now that they were so far from the base, was half a gallon, and a man, after a day in a tank, could drink half a gallon at a single draught if

115

he were foolish enough to do so. Half a gallon meant only just enough water to keep thirst from coming to close quarters; only the most fussy among the men would spare a cupful for shaving, and the days when the radiators had been extra thirsty, so that the men's rations were cut in half, were days of torment.

The major and the gunner and the driver settled down in the desert for their supper. Long habit had blunted the surprise the major had once felt at finding himself, a field officer, squatting in the dust with a couple of privates, and, fortunately, long habit had done the same for the privates. Before this campaign opened they would have been tongue-tied and awkward at his presence. It had not been easy to reach adjustment, but they had succeeded – as witness the way in which, without saying a word, they had caused him to leave off talking about eggs. He was still 'sir' to them, but almost the only other way in which his rank was noticeable in their personal relationships was that the two privates both suspected the major of being the guilty party in the matter of the loss of one of their three enamelled mugs. They had not ventured openly to accuse him, and he remained in ignorance of their suspicions, taking it for granted that the gunner – a scatter-brained fellow – had been at fault in the matter.

It was an infernal nuisance, being short of a mug; two mugs among three of them called for a whole lot of organisation, especially in the morning, when they had to clean their teeth, and sometimes to shave and sometimes to make tea – and the gunner liked his strong, and the driver liked his weak, and the major was the only one who did not want sugar in it. If ever the three of them were to quarrel, the major knew it would be over some difficulty arising out of the loss of the mug. Yet he did not see nowadays anything odd about a major worrying over the prospect of a disagreement with a couple of privates over an enamelled mug.

And tonight he was additionally lucky, because the rations for the day were a tinned meat and vegetable concoction that he particularly disliked. But the gunner and the driver were loud in their delight when they discovered what fate had brought them tonight. They ate noisily and appreciatively, while the major squatting beside them made only the merest pretence of eating and allowed his thoughts to stray back to memories of dinner at the Berkeley and the gargantuan lunches at Simpson's in the Strand. And also of eggs.

It was dark now, and cold – before supper was over the major had to reach out for a blanket and wrap it round his shoulders as the treacherous desert wind blew chilly. The stars were out, but there was no moon yet and the darkness was impenetrable. There was nothing to do now except sleep. The major chose himself a spot where the scrub grew not too thickly, and where the rock did not jut entirely through the thin skin of earth which overlaid it. He spread his blankets over his fleabag and crawled in with the dexterity of long practice without disturbing the arrangement. The bit of tarpaulin stretched from the side of the tank to the earth kept off the dew, if there should be any, and the joints that had suffered on the steel piano stool and on the steel roof snuggled gratefully against the more kindly contact of the earth. And long habit was a help.

He awoke in the middle of the night with a shattering roar in his very ear. The driver had his own system of keeping his beloved motor warm enough to start. He slept only under two blankets, and when the cold awoke him he knew that it was necessary to warm up the motor. He would crawl out of bed, start it up, allow it to run for five minutes, and then switch it off. That meant that the light tank was always ready for instant action, but the major had never been able to acquire the habit of sleeping through the din of the motor. The only habit he had been able to form was that of cursing to himself at the driver, feebly, half awake, and then of turning over and completing his night's sleep. The gunner, on the other hand, slept stolidly through the whole racket, snoring away stubbornly

— the major suspected him of dreaming about eggs.

Before dawn they were up and doing. Two inches of sand in the bottom of a petrol tin made an admirable wick; petrol soaked into it burned with an almost clear flame and heated the water for their tea in a flash. They had grown cunning lately and brushed their teeth after breakfast, using the remains of the tea for the purpose; that gave them an additional two swallows of water apiece to drink at the mid-morning halt for filling up. The motor started, shatteringly noisy as usual. Then they were off, the long line of tanks heaving and rolling over the desert, the familiar plumes of dust trailing behind them, the familiar weary ache beginning to grow in the joints of the major as he settled himself on the piano stool.

The major's calculation of his position was a hazy one, and through no fault of his own. Erratic compasses, ridiculous Italian maps and strict wireless silence combined, after a march hundreds of miles long, to make it very doubtful where they were. But the major was philosophic about it. British light tanks were capable of fighting almost anything in Africa, and what they could not fight they could run away from; they had learned that lesson in innumerable untold skirmishes in the old days of the beginning of the war. The major felt ready for anything that might happen, as he stared out through the slit of the conning tower across the yellowish brown plain.

Yet all the same it is doubtful if he was really ready for the sight that met his eyes. The tank came lurching and rolling up a sharp slope. It heaved itself over the crest — the note of the motor changing ever so little as the gradient altered — and a new landscape was presented to the major's eyes.

First of all he saw the sea, the blue sea, the wonderful blue sea, flecked with white. The major wriggled on the piano stool and yelled involuntarily at the top of his voice when he saw it. That marvellous horizon, that beautiful colour, that new-found sense of achievement and freedom — they were simply intoxicating. The driver and the gunner

118

were as intoxicated as he was, screwing their necks round to grin at him, the fluffy immature beard of the gunner wagging on his chin.

And then they cleared the next curve of the crest, and the major saw the road, that long coastal road for the construction of which Mussolini had poured out so much treasure. The major had expected to see it from the moment when he had seen the sea – in fact, he was craning his neck for a sight of it. But he was not ready for the rest of what he saw. For twenty miles the road was black with the fleeing Italian army – an enormous column of men and vehicles, jamming the road from side to side, hastening westward – Bergenzoli's army escaping from Benghazi and from the wrath of the English behind them. From a point nearly ahead of them away off to the right stretched that hurrying column. From his point of vantage the major could see it looping like some monstrous water snake along the curves of the road. Now he knew why his squadron had been hurled across the desert at such a frantic speed. It had been planned to cut off Bergenzoli's retreat, and the object had been achieved, with no more than ten minutes to spare.

Those ten minutes were only to spare if the major did the right thing on the instant. But twenty years of training had prepared the major for that very purpose. He was still a hussar, even though his squadron's horses had long ago been replaced by light tanks. His mental reactions were instantaneous; there was no need to stop and ponder the situation. The trained tactical eye took in the lie of the land even while he was shouting into the wireless transmitter the vital information that he was ahead of the Italians. He saw the road and the ridge beside it, and the moment that the information had been acknowledged he was speaking again, quietly already, giving his orders to the squadron. The long line of tanks wheeled and swooped down upon the road.

So close was the race that they were barely in position before the head of the column was up to them. An hour later and the Italians would have been able to post a flank guard behind whose shelter most of them would have been able to slip away. As it was, the major just had time to give his orders to his two troops as the head of the Italian column came down upon them.

The tanks bucked themselves into position and the machine guns spoke out, pouring their fire into the trucks packed with infantry which were so recklessly coming down upon them. It was slaughter, the dire punishment of a harebrained attack. The major watched the trucks swerve off the road, saw the startled infantry come tumbling out while the machine-gun fire cut swaths through them. Truck piled upon truck. The poor devils in them were deserving of pity. At one moment they had thought themselves safe, rolling along a good road back to Tripoli, and then the next these grey monsters had come darting out of the desert across their path, spraying death.

With the checking of the head of the column, confusion spread up the road. The major could see movement dying away as each successive section bumped up against the one ahead; the sudden outburst of firing, taking everyone by surprise, was rousing panic among the weaker individuals. So much the better. From the major's point of view, there could not be too much panic. Somewhere up that column there were field guns and there were heavy tanks, and to neither of them could he offer any real resistance. The more confusion there was in the column, the longer would it take to extricate these, the only weapons that could clear its path. Time was of the utmost importance; he turned and looked back over his shoulder at where the sun was dipping towards the horizon and the blue sea. This time, by some curious chance, his mind was in a condition to take in the fact that the approaching sunset would be red and lurid. He was smiling grimly as he turned back to his work.

Someone over there was trying to urge the unarmoured infantry to the attack – to certain death, in other words, in the face of the two grim little groups of tanks that

120

opposed them. Some of them came forward to the certain death too. And the sun was nearer the horizon.

Farther back down the column frantic officers were clearing a path for the artillery. There were eddies and swirls in the mass. Trucks were being heaved off the road as the guns came through. The major took his glasses from his eyes and gave another order. The tanks curvetted and wheeled, the next moment they had a ridge of solid earth between them and the guns. There was a dreary wait – the major had time for another glance at the sun sinking in a reddened sky – before the shells began to come over. Then the major could smile; they were shrieking over the crest and a good two yards above his head before they buried themselves in the ridge behind him. But there was infantry creeping forward again; there was still the chance that he might be forced sideways out of his position and have to leave a gap through which the mob might escape. He looked at the sun again, and then out to his right, the direction from which he had come, and he felt a glow of relief. The rest of the advance guard was coming – a battalion of motorised infantry with their battery of anti-tank guns. Now they had a chance. But where were the cruiser tanks, the only weapons in Africa that could stop the heavy tanks when they should be able to make their way out of the column?

It had been touch and go in the first place, when the light tanks had cut off the retreat of the column. It was touch and go now, when the light tanks and five hundred British soldiers were trying to stop the advance of fifty thousand Italians. But night was close at hand. Darkness blinded the Italian gunners and paralysed the efforts being made to clear the road for the heavy tanks. The major neatly withdrew his tanks over one more ridge, in case of a night attack – in all his extensive experience with the Italians they had never ventured a single operation in darkness – and went round his squadron to see that they were as well prepared as might be for a battle on the morrow.

The major always remembers that night as one when there was nothing he found it necessary to do. The British soldier was on the offensive. The veriest fool could see victory just ahead, victory of a crushing type, nothing less than annihilation of the enemy, if only the force of which the squadron formed a part could hold back Bergenzoli until pressure on his rear and the arrival of help to themselves should convince Bergenzoli of the hopelessness of his position. With victory depending on the proper lubrication of their tanks, on their precautions against surprise, they needed no telling, no inspection, to make them do their duty. The major was not an imaginative man, but something in his imagination was touched that night when he talked to his men. The final destruction of the Italians was what they had in mind; the fact that they would be opposed tomorrow by odds of a hundred to one, and that there was more chance of their being dead by evening than alive, did not alter their attitude in the least.

The major walked from one little group to another; the once-khaki overalls worn by everyone, even himself, had been bleached almost white by exposure, and the oil stains somehow did not darken them in a bad light, so that the men he spoke to showed up as ghostly figures in the darkness. There was laughter in the voices of the ghosts he spoke to – laughter and delight in the imminent prospect of victory. And in the stillness of the desert night they could hear, across two valleys, the din of the heavy Italian tanks roaring up to take up positions for the charge that would try to clear the way for the Italians next day. That was the lullaby the major heard as he stretched out in the desert to try to snatch a couple of hours' sleep, side by side with the driver and the gunner. Only in the grave did officers and men sleep side by side until this war came.

Dawn – the first faint light that precedes dawn – showed, looming over the farthest crest, the big Italian tanks which had been somehow forced forward along the tangled column during the night. They came forward ponderously, with fifty thousand men behind them, and in front of them there was only a thread of infantry, a single battery, a squadron of light tanks whose armour was only fit to keep out rifle bullets. It was as if the picadors and the matadors in the bull ring had to fight, not a single bull but a whole herd of bulls, all charging in the madness of desperation.

There is an art in the playing of a charging bull, even in the handling of a whole herd. Through a long and weary day, that was just what the major's squadron and the rest of the British force succeeded in doing. Since time immemorial – from Alexander to Hitler – it has been the fate of advance guards to be sacrificed to gain time for the manoeuvre of the main body, to be used to pin the enemy to the ground, so that his flank can be safely assailed. Only troops of the highest discipline and training can be trusted to fulfil such a mission, however. The Italian tanks which were recklessly handled were lured into the fire of the battery; the timid ones were prevailed upon to procrastinate. The slow retreat of the British force was over ground marked with crippled tanks and littered with Italian dead; and there were British dead there, too, and knocked-out British guns, and burned-out British tanks.

It was an exhausted British force that still confronted the Italians. The line had shrunk, so that on its left flank, towards the sea, there was an open gap through which, among the sand dunes, some of the Italians were beginning to dribble on foot, creeping along the edge of the sea in the wild hope of escaping captivity. And then, at that last moment, came the decisive blow. At least to us here it seems the last moment. That can only be a guess – no one dare say that the British had reached the end of their resistance. But it was at that moment, when British riflemen were fighting hard to protect their headquarters, when two-thirds of the British guns were out of action, when the major's squadron was reduced to three tanks, that help arrived. From out of the desert there came a sweeping line of huge British cruiser tanks. They came charging down on the Italian flank, enormous, invulnerable and terrifying. It is impossible to guess at the miracle of organisation, at the prodigy of hard work, which had brought these monstrous things across sands which had scarcely even been trodden by camels.

From out of the desert they came, wreathed in dust, spouting fire, charging down upon the tangled mass of the Italian army pent back behind the thin dam of the British line. The Italian tanks wheeled to meet them, and then and there the battle was fought out, tank to tank, under the brazen sky, over the sand where the dead already lay. The dust clouds wrapped them round, dimming the bright flames – visible even in the sunshine – which streamed from the wrecked tanks, the Viking pyres of their slain crews.

When it was over, the whole battle was finished. There was no fight left in the Italians. The desert had already vomited out three fierce attacks – first the major's light tanks, then the infantry, and last the cruiser tanks, and no one could guess what next would come forth. And from the rear came the news that the pursuing British were pressing on the rear guard; at any moment the sea might bring its quota of death, should the British ships find a channel through the sandbanks which would bring their guns within range of the huddled army. Front, rear and both flanks were open to attack, and overhead the air force was about to strike. Nor was that all. Thirst was assailing them, those unhappy fifty thousand men massed without a single well within reach. There was nothing for it but surrender.

The major watched the fifty thousand men yield up their arms; he knew that he was witness to one of the great victories of history, and he was pleased about it. Through the dreadful fatigue that was overwhelming him he also was aware that he had played a vital part in the gaining of that victory, and that somewhere in the future there would be mentions in dispatches and decorations. But his eyelids were heavy and his shoulders drooping.

Then came the gunner; his faded, oil-stained overalls

124

made more shocking than ever by the stains of the blood of the wounded driver, and that horribly fluffy yellow beard of his, like the down on a baby chick, offending the sunlight. Now that they had reached the sea, the distillation plants would supply them with a sufficiency of water and that beard could be shaved off. But the gunner was grinning all over his face, his blue eyes nearly lost in the wrinkles round them, lines carved by the blinding light of the desert. The gunner had heard a cock crowing down beside the solitary white farmhouse towards the sea on the edge of the battlefield, and he had walked there and back on stiff legs. The gunner held out a big fist before the major, and opened the fingers like a man doing a conjuring trick. In his hand was an egg.

The Dumb Dutchman

When the German police came aboard the *Lek II* that May morning at Düsseldorf, Jan Schuylenboeck thought that they had found out about his activities, and he set his hand to the pocket where his pencil was; concealed beneath the rubber eraser at the end of that pencil was enough poison to insure for him a death much more rapid than the Gestapo would allow him. But it turned out that there was no immediate need for the poison, because the arrival of the police was not the first step in a personal tragedy; it was part of a national tragedy, of a world-wide tragedy, for that was the morning that the Germans invaded Holland, and the police were arresting, not a spy – which Schuylenboeck had been for a long time – but an enemy alien; Schuylenboeck had been that for only a few minutes, after the German planes had dropped their first bombs on the Dutch civilian population.

The *Lek II* was a tugboat, almost new; since long before the war began between Germany and England, Schuylenboeck, as her owner and captain, had been taking vast tows up the Rhine to supply the German war machine. It had been a profitable contract, but the money had been no sort of compensation to the tug's captain; instead, he had found his reward in reporting to London all the numerous things that a tugboat captain can discover during voyages to the German munition towns on the Rhine.

The police officer was quite apologetic about arresting Jan Schuylenboeck; odd though it was for a Gestapo man

126

to be apologetic about anything at all.

'The purest formality, Captain,' said the police officer. 'We are under orders to arrest every Dutchman and Belgian in the country. But I am quite sure that it was not meant to include you, because you have been known too long as a friend of the party. A pity that you did not join along with your brother-in-law, but in any case, I am sure you will soon be released. We cannot spare either you or the *Lek II* for long.'

'I am glad to hear that,' said Schuylenboeck.

Years of practice had already taught him never to allow his expression to change, never to say anything that might betray him. The fact that his hated brother in-law had for some time been a member of the Dutch Nazi Party had been of considerable use to him, even though it had not made his life any happier. Schuylenboeck kept his face expressionless while the radio poured out its tremendous news – of how the German army was pouring almost unchecked over two frontiers; of the breaking of the Belgian defence line on the Albert Canal by a panzer division from Aachen; of the descent of parachute troops everywhere, forestalling the cutting of the dykes, which might have let in the sea and saved the country; and later on, the news of the bombing of Rotterdam and the surrender of the Dutch army. Schuylenboeck could not manage to make himself appear pleased at the news that both the Netherlands and Belgium were conquered, that France was tumbling into ruin, but at the same time he managed to conceal his delight at the news that the British army had escaped at Dunkirk. Everybody knew him as a stolid, stodgy Dutchman, and violent demonstrations were not expected of him.

Even before the Dutch surrender, arrangements had already been made to continue Schuylenboeck and the *Lek II* in the employment of the Third Reich. Now there were huge quantities of loot to be got out of the prostrate country. For a time, until the Dutch should be reduced to utter misery, the shipments up the Rhine would be heavier than ever. Schuylenboeck nodded when he was told. He could not trust himself ever to speak, it seemed to him.

And yet, when the time came and he met that brother-in-law of his whom he had always disliked so intensely, the one who had been a Nazi for years, he nerved himself to be quite cordial to him.

'I'm glad to hear you've made up your mind to co-operate, Jan,' said Braun.

'It's the only logical thing to do,' grunted Schuylen-boeck.

'Exactly. Look at me. Head of a whole district already. When peace comes and the New Order is fully established, I shall be the ruler of thousands, millions. And meanwhile – meanwhile I have enough to eat and plenty of money to spend. It will be the same for you.'

'So it seems.'

'The people think they're very clever, not speaking to me. You'll find the same thing, but don't let it worry you. I'll attend to that. Old Mrs Honig – she's some relation to me, you know – didn't invite me to the party to celebrate her golden wedding. Didn't invite me, although I'm her cousin, and in my official position. To tell the truth, I have an idea that she started the idea of a golden wedding party just so as to be able not to invite me. Well, much good it did her and her doddering old husband. I suppose you've heard where they spent their precious golden wedding.'

'Yes, I've heard,' said Schuylenboeck. He automatically fingered his beloved pencil with the dose of poison hidden under the eraser. If he were ever in danger of being sent to the same place, the poison would be useful. A pity that the old Honigs had not had such a poison in their possession when they were arrested.

Four times the *Lek II* and her captain took big tows of loot up the Rhine for delivery in the industrial towns. On one occasion the British bombers raided Ruhrort while Schuylenboeck was there, and one bomb burst on the quay not very far from the *Lek II*, and started a beautiful fire among the very stores she had brought up the river. Schuylenboeck thought to himself how glad the people to whom he used to report would have been to receive that piece of news. But Schuylenboeck had no intention at all of risking detection in order to convey what would be, after all, a very minor piece of news. He was saving himself for something more important than that; he did not know what, but he thought the opportunity would come one of these days – that is, unless he was compelled to use the dose of poison which lay concealed under the eraser in his pencil. If that bomb had hit the *Lek II* and killed Schuylenboeck at that time, the fading memory of him would have been merely that of one more of the few pitiful traitors who betrayed the Netherlands.

And then came a change of duties to Schuylenboeck and a change of scene for the *Lek II*. The long journeys up the Rhine – somehow pleasant despite the torrent of unhappy memories which they evoked – ended for good. It was not because there was no more loot to be extracted from Holland; there was still plenty, but it could be entrusted to tug masters of less ability and less reliability than Schuylenboeck.

Flushing was a scene of boiling activity. For the defensive – to guard against an English attack – there were minefields being laid and big guns being mounted and concrete blockhouses being erected. For the offensive there was a German army to be trained in embarkation and debarkation; also there was a motley flotilla of tugs and lighters and shallow-draft steamers to be trained in the same operations.

Schuylenboeck had often devoted some of his thoughts to the problem facing the Germans of invading England. To start with, there was the question of obtaining, even temporarily, the command of the sea. Schuylenboeck dismissed that from his mind; the Nazis might by some astonishing combination of circumstances be able to bypass it. But after that came the question of ferrying over a large number of men and a huge mass of material. Schuylenboeck could make calculations about that; he had spent his life dealing with questions of water transport. Before his eyes here in Flushing he could see some of the steps the Nazis were taking to solve the problem. First he scratched his head, with its thinning straw-coloured hair, and then, finding little inspiration in that, he pulled at his fat pink cheeks and stared out over the crowded harbour, narrowing his eyelids over his slightly protuberant blue eyes. He was not a handsome man, nor did he appear to be a particularly intellectual man. And certainly he did not appear to be a man who could evolve and cherish through months of intense danger a deep design.

About a hundred men to a lighter, Schuylenboeck saw that the Nazis were allowing. What would be the total force they would try to employ? Schuylenboeck had little idea, but he fixed arbitrarily upon three hundred thousand. That meant three thousand lighters. That meant – Schuylenboeck was not good at mental arithmetic, but he dared not risk putting such calculations on paper – a string of lighters one hundred and fifty miles long if in single file, taking about twenty hours to pass a given point at their best speed – doubtful when there were intricate channels through shoals and minefields to be traversed. But of course every harbour from Emden down to Cherbourg, or beyond, would be employed. Then came the question of equipment, of tanks and guns. Schuylenboeck groaned in misery at the thought of all those unknown quantities intruding themselves into his calculations. He had no idea how much space they would require. Schuylenboeck was reminded of the little boy who asked his father how much a million pennies made and, being told that it made the devil of a lot of money, got into trouble next morning in school because it was the wrong answer.

The Nazis had the devil of a problem on their hands – a problem depending on the utmost nicety of timing, on the most accurate planning, on the most careful consideration of navigational conditions of tides and wind. And he was well aware that they were doing their usual painstak-

130

ing best to eliminate all the possible unknowns.

Colonel Potthoff was in charge of the embarkation arrangements in the Flushing sector. Schuylenboeck came to know him well, a man almost as bulky as Schuylenboeck himself, with a good deal of the bulk protruding over the back of his collar in naked, fleshy rolls. Potthoff used to sit at his desk in the harbour-master's office and wheeze heavily over timetables.

'Six hours for the troops to file into the lighters, Major Roth!' said Potthoff. 'That is too much. Then four more to get the lighters clear of the mole. Quite impossible . . . Captain Schuylenboeck, you must see to it the lighters get to sea quicker than that.'

'Yes, sir,' said Schuylenboeck and Roth dutifully; presumably, Roth's tone was sincere.

It was an intricate, difficult job to arrange the troops, on the word being given, to march out of their barracks and take their position in order in the waiting lighters – the harbour was chock-a-block with them – and then make up the tows and get them out of the harbour through the narrowed entrance. Nor was the situation eased by the fact that half of the tug masters were Dutch and did their best unobtrusively to muddle the business; the captain of a tug with six lighters in tow can cause a quite amazing tangle if he is so inclined. There was one Dutch captain who managed to get his tow into the minefield outside the entrance and blow one lighter of troops to fragments. But the Germans shot him, even though he pleaded that it was an unavoidable accident.

Schuylenboeck approved of the blowing up of the lighter, but he never indulged in the petty obstructionism of the other captains. He was hoping, deep down in the stolid bulk of him, for larger game. His helpfulness in the matter of manoeuvring tows won him still further the confidence of his Nazi tyrants; it won him the responsibility of handling a tow of no fewer than ten lighters – the *Lek II*'s fullest capacity – and it won him the hatred of all those who had once been his friends. Schuylenboeck was reduced to drinking his evening beer – thin wartime stuff – in the company of his brother-in-law, Braun, eyed askance by the loyalists. There were small compensations; Braun still had a stock of the thin Sumatra cigars with a straw up the middle that Schuylenboeck loved, and he told Schuylenboeck scraps of information that Schuylenboeck stored up in his mind, ready to tell when the time should come, if he did not have to use the poison under the eraser first.

It was not only in embarkation that the Nazi troops had to be drilled. They also had to practise disembarkation. The tows, when they had crept out as far to sea as they dared, turned about and headed for shore again; there to practise, some of them, running aground in the shallows, where the troops leaped out waist deep and poured up the beaches, and some to practise running alongside the jetty in what, for the purposes of the manoeuvre, was assumed to be a captured port. There were times when the Royal Air Force came over, raining bombs, and with the fighters spouting 20-mm. shells, wreaking destruction on the flotilla and killing the hapless soldiers in the lighters. Yet after each such attack, more lighters crept round from the German shipbuilding yards, more troops came to fill the gaps, and the rehearsal went steadily on. And during this dreadful August, when the RAF was fighting to preserve England from Goering's bombers, there was not much strength to spare to harass the invasion forces.

August shifted into September. Still the bombers roared overhead on their way to raid London, and still they came limping back in diminished numbers. The days were growing shorter, the nights longer. And Schuylenboeck still waited, imperturbable, for his opportunity, whatever that opportunity might be; his gesture towards his breast pocket where his pencil had by now become quite habitual to him.

It was Colonel Rücker's engineer regiment, the 79th Pioneers, which was allotted to the *Lek II*'s tow. Colonel

Rücker was one of those fierce, conscientious soldiers with an infinity of training who have helped to make the German army what it is. The Nazis have worked out a system which puts the engineer regiments in the forefront of the battle; the way to every victory is cleared by the pioneers. Rücker was the man who had first set foot in Eben Emael and struck the first blow in the campaign which was to carry the Germans from the Rhine to the Pyrenees. The lines on his face made him look older than his thirty-eight years, and if one looked closely at his shorn head one could see plenty of grey hairs, but he still carried himself with a spring and an elasticity which would have been a credit to a boy of half his years. The 79th Pioneers, hardbitten veterans, all of them, were waiting for their chance to head the landing force that would march on London just as they had marched on Paris. In those early weeks of the war against England, left single-handed, there was no doubt in their minds that the enterprise would succeed, just as every other enterprise had succeeded up to that time; the disappointments for the German army still lay in the future.

That September day the orders came through early in the morning, and the German army came pouring out from its billets and its barracks, and marching in from the outlying suburbs with the regularity to be expected of a disciplined army after a dozen rehearsals. The motor vehicles came roaring along the quay and down the ramps laid down for them – five armoured cars and five light tanks, one for each of the ten lighters in the *Lek II*'s train. Simultaneously came the 79th Pioneers, marching swiftly in column of threes and taking their places in the lighters in mechanical obedience to the unhurried orders of the non-commissioned officers.

Colonel Rücker and the regimental headquarters took their places in the leading lighter; Rücker was aware that it would be more dignified for him to stand on the bridge of the tug, but the *Lek II* drew far more water than the lighters, and it was the lighters that would run ashore under their own impetus after the tug had cast them off. On board the *Lek II* there came only Krauss, the assistant signalling officer, and a couple of privates, ready to receive any communication which Colonel Rücker might see fit to make.

As the last man stepped aboard, the warps were cast off, and Schuylenboeck, with a last glance round him from the bridge, rang down for slow speed ahead. With infinite slowness, lest a sudden jerk should snap the tow ropes, the tow was under way, circled and headed for the harbour mouth; even as it moved, fresh barges were being warped into their places and fresh troops were marching down on to the quay, ready to embark. Still moving slowly, the *Lek II* and her lumbering train passed out into the open sea, almost glass smooth, and with a dim sun looking down upon it. Overhead at that moment there passed a vast diamond of bombers, the fighter escort so tiny as almost to be lost in the faint haze, heading for England. The war in the air was being fought out to its climax while war on land was still in rehearsal.

'A nice calm day,' said Lieutenant Krauss benignly. The slightest lop on the water, even such as would not prevent the unseaworthy barges from carrying out their exercises, was enough to make him seasick and miserable.

'A beautiful day,' agreed Schuylenboeck heartily.

He looked up at the dim sun and at the haze-shrouded horizon, and then hastily, in fear lest even that gesture should have betrayed his thoughts, at the rest of the barges jockeying their way out of the harbour. And lest he had betrayed himself, he felt in his pocket for the reassurance of his pencil. He knew much more about the Narrow Seas than did Lieutenant Krauss; he knew what kind of weather that glassy sea and indistinct horizon portended. Right ahead, for that matter, he was almost sure he could see a hint of the fogbank he was hoping for.

Despite Colonel Potthoff's complaints, it still took a most unconscionable time for the whole flotilla to get clear of the harbour mouth and the minefields beyond.

The *Lek II* chugged slowly ahead while the rest of the flotilla emerged and took up its formation; in that formation the *Lek II* was still destined to be ahead for the 79th Pioneers to make the first landing. But time today was not of so much importance, for when the embarkation rehearsal was completed, the force was destined to turn leisurely about – and with that agglomerate mass of barges every tiny movement had to be leisurely made – and return to the shore after nightfall to practise a night landing. Slowly the flotilla headed out to sea, until almost beyond the protection of the heavy shore batteries. Farther ahead still were to be seen the dim shapes of the light cruiser and the half-flotilla of destroyers which guarded against some unforeseen eruption of the British light forces. Dimmer and dimmer grew those shapes; soon a little wreath of fog, twisting sluggishly over the water, came athwart the *Lek II*'s bows and was cut by them into halves. There was no heat to the pale sun now; within a few minutes there was no sun to be seen, and the destroyer screen on the horizon was entirely invisible.

One of the privates on the bridge beside Krauss and Schuylenboeck suddenly called attention to the tow; a signaller in the leading barge was sending a message by semaphore, and Krauss read it off with the ease of long practice. 'We are to go back without carrying out the night landing,' said Krauss, and Schuylenboeck nodded ponderously and rang down for full speed ahead.

'What are you doing that for?' asked Krauss curiously, noting the quickened beat of the propeller.

'It is necessary to go faster in order to lead round on the curve,' explained Schuylenboeck without emotion.

Further wreaths of fog were curling past them now, and a moment later they had reached the fogbank. From the bridge of the *Lek II* it was impossible to see even the bows of the tug. The people in the barges would not be able to see the tug ahead or the barge behind. Schuylenboeck gave a slight alteration of course to the man at the wheel, and five minutes later a much larger one in the opposite direction. That was sufficient to put confusion into Krauss' mind, and possibly into the helmsman's. They were headed for England now by the shortest route, but only Schuylenboeck was aware of it; he had no intention at all, and never had, of taking any of the crew into his confidence. When one lives under Nazi rule one takes no one into one's confidence.

The fog was clammy and chill; Krauss began to pace the little bridge to keep himself warm; after the beautiful weather of August, 1940, he was a little susceptible to cold. But Schuylenboeck stood there unmoving, his hand, in its characteristic attitude, resting over his inside breast pocket. He was aware of the importance of showing no sign of nervousness.

Then, just ahead, a slightly more solid nucleus of the grey fog flicked past the *Lek II*'s bows; it was come and gone in a flash, but Schuylenboeck felt the *Lek II* pitch a little under his feet as she met the resultant wash. That was one of the German destroyers, and they were through the screen now, with nothing hostile between them and England, unless some dreadful coincidence – Schuylenboeck felt for his pencil again – should guide them into contact with a lurking U-boat. Schuylenboeck ordered another small alteration of course, kept to it for half an hour, and then, to anticipate Krauss' inevitable restlessness, he bellowed an order forward for a hand to go to work with the lead. That would look as if he were expecting to approach shore at any moment, and the five fathoms which the leadsman got was, as he had anticipated, the tail of the Camelbank. Schuylenboeck discontinued the heaving of the lead immediately; he did not want deep water reported.

Half an hour more of this. That was the utmost limit of time he dared to allow himself. Krauss was restless by now, and far back in the fog he could guess that Colonel Rücker was also growing restless. They ought to have made the harbour mouth an hour back. It was fortunate that, having started at the head of the procession, they would return at the tail, so that there was nothing very surprising about their having seen nothing of the other tows; and Schuylenboeck, ponderously working out a psychological problem, could guess that Rücker, with his vast experience of war and of the confusion resulting even in a well-drilled army like the German at an unexpected change of conditions, would expect a certain amount of delay, and would rely, in his disciplined German fashion, on the judgement of the man on the spot.

Schuylenboeck nerved himself to speak; it was one thing to be his usual ponderous self and quite another to have to say words like an actor.

'I shall have to send a radio call,' he said to Krauss. 'Then I can pick up my bearings with the direction finder.'

'Very good,' said Krauss. Schuylenboeck's blue eyes noted the fact that Krauss was nervous, but not yet suspicious. What he was afraid of was the minefields, and the possibility of bumping into the breakwater or running down another tow. Schuylenboeck scribbled the message on the pad and handed it to Joris Hohlwerff in the little radio room beside the chartroom. He had no knowledge at all as to whether young Joris was a willing co-operator or not. 'Co-operator' in the conquered countries has the special meaning of a man who has taken the German side. If he had been sure that Joris was not one, Schuylenboeck might have sent a very different message, but under Nazi rule one is sure of nothing. The hiss and crackle of the transmission showed that Joris was dispatching the message, and the British kept a ceaseless wireless watch, and they had direction finders as well.

A precious ten minutes passed – another mile nearer England – before Joris came out with the reply sent out by a puzzled German station.

'Repeat my message,' order Schuylenboeck. He met Joris' eyes with a stony stare, and Joris' stare was just as stony. Neither of these men knew anything at all about what was passing in the other's mind. But the transmission

137

hissed and crackled. The British navy must be picking up those waves.

Far out here in the North Sea there was a perceptible movement of the water. The *Lek II* was positively lively and the lighters astern must be lurching disgustingly. Schuylenboeck hoped that Rücker would be too sick to be suspicious. It was twenty minutes now since the first wireless message. Any British destroyer taking it in ten miles away could be here by now to investigate. To convey an attitude of activity, Schuylenboeck began ringing down messages to the engine room for half speed, for slow speed ahead, for half speed again. Lieutenant Krauss, beside him, marvelled at the assurance of this experienced tug master who could bring a great tow into port with such a sureness of touch in a fog that limited visibility to twenty yards. Krauss still had not the least idea that he was forty miles out in the North Sea instead of being at the entrance to Flushing.

Joris, his face as expressionless as before, brought out on the pad a most indignant message. This time it was from an admiral. He simply could not understand what had come over the *Lek II*, and demanded that she turn about and come home at once by the aid of directional wireless. Schuylenboeck wrote out the longest message of apology that he could think of and suggested that the cause of it all was compass failure. He would, of course, obey orders immediately. That would gain time, and would continue to help the British navy in its search, and would postpone any dispatch of German destroyers in pursuit. The fastest German destroyer, leaving immediately, would not be up to them for more than an hour. Schuylenboeck quitted his hold on his poison pencil long enough to look at his watch, while Joris sent his reply, and then, at his captain's order, repeated it for good measure.

Then at last it happened, the appearance of a vague shape through the mist and a bellowed challenge through a megaphone. The words spoken were English, but Schuylenboeck had schooled himself for so long to be

138

without emotion that he felt no relief, standing still while Krauss leaped excitedly to the rail to stare at the menacing grey silhouette. The destroyer, her guns trained, rolled heavily in the swell almost on top of the *Lek II*.

'Who the hell are you?' demanded the English voice again, irritation and curiosity intermingled in its tone.

'Dutch tug *Lek Two*!' roared Schuylenboeck back.

The relative motions of the ships carried them past each other, although Schuylenboeck had rung down immediately to stop the engines. So close were they that Schuylenboeck could hear the words being spoken on the destroyer's deck, and the exclamation of surprise as the English sighted the first of the lighters in tow.

From Colonel Rücker's lighter there came a sudden splutter of machine-gun fire. Rücker was a quick thinker, had recognised the English destroyer for what she was, and had put his men's guns into action. But it did not last long, because the British ship's guns made instant reply. Fifty-pound shells at point-blank range tore into the fragile barge, and it broke in the centre. Colonel Rücker and the leading half-company of the 79th Pioneers met their end there in the mist-shrouded water. The rest of the regiment surrendered – nine lighters, nine hundred men fully equipped for the invasion of England, five light tanks and four armoured cars.

'That was a good show,' said the lieutenant-commander to Schuylenboeck, as they sat down in the tiny cabin abaft the destroyer's bridge.

Schuylenboeck sat down heavily. He could not throw off all in a minute the forced immobility of expression which he had added to his natural immobility. He could not even show relief; he could not even drop the old gesture of fumbling with his pencil in his breast pocket. A thought struck him; for the sake of something to do while searching for words, he took the pencil out. He would not need the poison now. With his thick fingers he pried the eraser out of its thin metal holder. The two little pills did not roll out, not even when he tapped the pencil. He

139

peered into the holder and it was empty. For a long time now – how long he could never know – he had been clinging to the wrong pencil.

'What a nerve you must have!' said the lieutenant-commander admiringly. Then he looked at the Dutchman's face again, and it was as white as paper, and the big hands were trembling violently.

'Thank God you came!' said Schuylenboeck. His lips were trembling, too, and all his big solid face seemed as though it was melting, collapsing, and there was sweat pouring down the heavy cheeks.

'Thank God you came!' repeated Schuylenboeck, and the lieutenant-commander was inclined ignorantly to revise his estimate.

If Hitler had Invaded England

The title tells you what this story is about. So often it has
been said, if Hitler had made the attempt to invade
Britain after the evacuation of Dunkirk, he would have
won the war, that it is worth analysing his chances. He
must be given in this narrative every possible chance, but
none of the impossible ones. Before war began he had
made no plans, and certainly no preparations, for the
invasion of Britain; if he had, history would have taken a
different course from that moment. If he had begun to
build a fleet of landing craft in 1938, for instance, the
British attitude at Munich might well have been different,
and certainly British re-armament would have been more
rapid. And it must be remembered that with the German
economy at full stretch for war production, such a fleet
could only have been built at the cost of a diminished
output of planes or guns or tanks or submarines.

With the outbreak of war, and even after the destruction of Poland, the same arguments apply. A life-and-
death campaign awaited him in France and the Low
Countries; until the defeat of France was certain, he could
spare nothing for any other venture. Even Hitler's optimistic intuition did not envisage a victory as cheap and
as rapid as the one he actually achieved, and we know
now that even after Dunkirk every available man and
machine was earmarked for the final assault upon France.
A more brilliant general, or one gifted with even more

141

acute intuition than Hitler's, might nevertheless have realised that it was not necessary to let loose all his forces to complete the overthrow of France, and might have held back some divisions and squadrons to prepare for the earliest possible attack upon England.

As Hitler himself pointed out, time was on England's side. Every day that went by afforded the British troops that had been brought back from the Continent a greater chance to recover, to reorganise and, at least to some extent, to rearm. The evacuation from Dunkirk continued until June 4, 1940. The end of September would bring weather conditions that would make invasion impossible; but by the end of September England already had a garrison large enough and well enough trained to make invasion utterly disastrous in any case.

Hitler's best chance was to strike at the earliest possible moment, to start his preparations the instant Dunkirk fell. He could not await the result of the Battle of Britain, for he was defeated in that battle, nor was it decided until September. He had to do everything at once; he had to hurl a minimum force against France; he had to scrape together the means of transporting the remainder across the Channel; and that meant that he had to think quickly enough to stop the remains of his navy, already weakened by its losses in the Norwegian campaign, from sailing on its luckless second excursion to Narvik – it actually sailed on that fatal fourth of June. He had to plan, train and execute. He had to make the best use of every possible moment. And if he had done so? Let us see.

I

The smoke was still lying along the edge of the sea, obscuring the beaches and the harbour, as the German troops came cautiously forward, past the burning buildings, among the littered dead, to receive the surrender of the last few British troops, of the last few thousand French troops, who had covered the miraculous withdrawal. The wrecks still smouldered in the shallows; the wounded still lay beside the sea wall blanched and dying. And the prisoners had fought a ten-day battle without rest. They were spiritless – not only because defeat had taken the heart out of them but also because they had reached the limit of fatigue. Weariness made them shamble rather than march; weariness bowed their heads and bent their shoulders.

It was a German major-general commanding panzer troops who wrote the report that changed the course of history. Brilliant soldier though he was, quick-witted, brave, thrusting, fearless of responsibility, he nevertheless had that cold military mind which could not understand the working of other minds. He stood up in his command car and looked, analytically and yet without sympathy, at the spiritless column, and he felt only contempt. When he sat down an hour later to write his report, that contempt still persisted and was evident in every word he wrote.

It was late in the morning, as was Hitler's custom, that he emerged from his sleeping room. At his appearance the staff officers in the operations room ceased their work on the maps where they were marking the present situation and sprang stiffly to attention. Hitler briefly acknowledged their salutes and hurried to the central table with its huge map.

'Well?' he demanded.

Von Brauchitsch was at his side in a flash.

'The last resistance has ceased at Dunkirk, *mein Führer,*' he said. 'The only British soldiers left are prisoners.'

'The Battle of Belgium has ended in total victory, *mein Führer,*' said Keitel.

'*Sieg heil!*' someone cried, and the cry was instantly taken up by the others. '*Sieg heil! Sieg heil!*'

Hitler stood bathing in the enthusiasm as a man might bathe in sunshine; as the cheering died away Keitel, the toady, added a further contribution to the congratulations.

'The last report describes the British army as utterly

demoralised,' he said, and turned and snapped at an officer behind him. 'Where's that final report from Dunkirk?'

The officer hastened out to find it, while Hitler glanced down at the map again, to look up at once with a question. 'Any activity on the part of the French army?'

'None, *mein Führer*,' answered Von Brauchitsch. 'Kluge and Hoth and Manstein are ready to attack.'

'And the French are ready to collapse,' replied Hitler meditatively.

At this moment the staff officer re-entered the room and handed the report to Keitel; Hitler observed the action and gave an inquiring glance.

'This is the relevant paragraph of the report, *mein Führer*,' said Keitel. ' "The appearance of the prisoners confirmed the impression that the greatest demoralisation exists in the enemy forces. Preliminary questioning indicates that they are convinced the war is lost." '

'So?' said Hitler, meditatively still. 'The British capitalists are feeling the impact of war at last. And now?' Suddenly he reached a decision; his extended hand clenched into a fist, and the fist struck the table a blow which echoed in the quiet room. 'We will move against England this moment,' he said. 'What's the need of a hundred and thirty divisions to conquer France? We can spare a dozen. We can spare twenty to follow up a beaten enemy. Mark them off, Van Brauchitsch. That one – that one – that one. Eleven infantry divisions. Those two panzer corps.'

'Two panzer corps, *mein Führer*?' questioned Von Brauchitsch deprecatingly.

'We can spare them. Take Von Rundstedt out of the line to command them. Give the rest of his army group to List. Von Rundstedt can begin to make his plans for the invasion of England from this moment. I want those divisions to start moving to the coast today. Assign Sperrle and the Third Air Fleet –'

'A whole air fleet, *mein Führer*?'

'You heard what I said! I want plans from Sperrle instantly. Tell Goering. Send for Raeder – he must go to

144

work at once. Keitel, Jodl, I want a *Führer* Order drawn up for my signature. I want my army to enter London within three weeks.'

'London!' echoed a voice. The whole staff was standing transfixed and silent, staring at the man whose intuition had brought him to a decision which might change the fate of all mankind. It was a scene that would never fade from their memory.

NEW ATTACK LAUNCHED UPON FRANCE, said the headline for anxious Englishmen to read, but in Wilhelmshaven Admiral Lütjens on the bridge of the *Gneisenau* received a message brought him by his breathless chief of staff. It took him only a moment to read, and only a moment longer to decide what to do about it.

'Make this signal,' he ordered. 'Cancel all preparations for sailing.'

'So the second Narvik expedition ends before it has begun, sir?' asked the chief of staff.

'Apparently so.'

'What are they going to do with us instead, do you think, sir?'

'We are not sailing north. Perhaps we'll be sailing south,' answered Lütjens.

GERMAN ONSLAUGHT WITH MASSES OF TANKS, said the headline, but in the river harbour in Magdeburg a fat and elderly barge captain came stumping out of the barge company's office back to the *Fritz Reuter*, where his mate and the other hand were at work opening the hatches.

'You can start putting those back, my boys,' he said, tapping one hand with the folded instructions he held in the other. 'Berlin's not for us. We go empty to Düsseldorf.'

'Empty to Düsseldorf?' repeated the mate stupidly.

'That's the word. And it's good-bye to Gretchen for a month or two. Further orders at Düsseldorf.'

FRESH GERMAN MASSES FLUNG IN, said the headline.

But that day a German infantry division came marching into Ostend, with bands playing and the commanding general standing on the corner of the *place* receiving the salute of the units as they tramped by him. They were well-disciplined troops, and as they marched at attention they kept their eyes to the front; it was only when they began to disperse to their billets that the chatter burst out uncontrolled.

'Ostend! I always said that was where we were going to.'

'Little Klein who always knows everything.'

'But what the devil are we *doing* here?' demanded another. 'We ought to be moving on Paris.'

'Oh, to hell with it.'

Lacklustre eyes had watched the division marching in. Small interest had been displayed by the inhabitants at this new incursion of the grey-uniformed conquerors. Nevertheless, one inconspicuous old man had stood at the roadside watching idly, his glance straying casually enough from uniform to uniform, from badge to badge. He was just an old man, too feeble apparently to be of any danger to anyone, but his feeble fingers could still tap a key, just for a few brief seconds, a code word and a number, word and number repeated once to make sure. It was the shortest message possible, far too brief to be picked up by the German counter-espionage, which was only now settling down to its duties. The air was crowded with a thousand messages as the battle went on that laid a great nation in the dust; this one reached its destination.

GERMANS REACH THE SEINE! said the headline, and the British public began to foresee that the conquest of Belgium would be followed by the conquest of France.

While that headline was being read, an acrimonious meeting was being conducted between two staffs, half a dozen German naval officers arguing with half a dozen officers of the Luftwaffe.

'This is the line,' said the naval captain. 'Cherbourg to Worthing.'

A map of the English Channel lay before them, and over the water surface of it were ruled two thick black lines, inclining steeply towards each other. The other ran from Hook of Holland to Deal.

'A hundred and sixty kilometres,' said the Luftwaffe colonel. 'Preposterous. To mine that line means two thousand sorties. In two thousand sorties we can bomb England into surrender. I have to inform you, sir, officially, that my chief thinks this whole plan not only costly and dangerous but quite unnecessary.'

'And I must remind you, sir,' said the captain, 'that these plans are being made as a result of a direct *Führer* Order. Your chief can carry his protests to the *Führer*, but you and I, sir, must plan the invasion of England.'

THE BATTLE FOR PARIS, said the headline. This was the day when the British public began to lose hope that 1940 would repeat the events of 1914 and produce another Miracle of the Marne. This was the day when one Englishman would say to another, 'It looks as if we'll have to go it alone.' But this was also the day when many Englishmen, looking back on the fiasco of Narvik, on the overrunning of Holland, on the collapse of Belgium and the evacuation from Dunkirk, could now contemplate the approaching fall of France – which would leave England absolutely alone and with neither responsibilities nor friends in Europe – and yet could answer, 'Well, I can't say I'm sorry.'

Then came the speeches of the prime minister, trumpet calls that gave guidance to the passionate and voiceless patriots who peopled England, unifying their determination and giving shape and frame to their hope.

Yet it was not to be expected that the staff officers in Brussels, hard-working and painstaking though they were, could spare a moment to listen to those trumpet calls. On the wall in that headquarters in Brussels hung an immense map, the large-scale ordnance maps of the southern counties of England, reproduced from the examples stored away in the files of Military Intelligence in Berlin and joined together so that the whole wall – one of the long walls of a Belgian gymnasium – was hardly big enough to hold the complete map. Looking at the map, each with a pointer in his hand, were a major-general and a colonel. They were chiefs of staff, the one to an army, the other to the parachute troops. At their elbows stood half a dozen junior officers, with notebooks and fountain pens in hand, ready to record decisions reached by their superiors.

'You've studied the trend of the ground,' said the major-general, with a sweep of his pointer.

'Yes,' said the colonel doubtfully. Beyond that he would not express his feelings in words, lest he be suspected of a lack of resolution in the shedding of blood – German blood, not that of the enemy, naturally. But the major-general was sensitive to the implications of the tone in which the word was uttered.

'What's your available strength as of today?' he demanded.

'Five thousand one hundred and fifty parachute troops,' answered the colonel promptly. 'Eleven thousand four hundred airborne troops who have completed training. There's another division, as you know, commencing training.'

'Not nearly as many as I should like,' commented the major-general. Was there a hint of disapproval in his voice?

'What is your information about the enemy's dispositions?' asked the colonel, making a subtle counter-attack successfully, as was proved by the length of time the major-general took to consider his answer.

'Not too detailed,' he answered at length, grudgingly. 'It isn't easy to get information from the island. Churchill arrested half our agents last week, and contact with the others is bound to be difficult.'

'The navy and the general want us to seize a harbour,' said the colonel. 'What about these places – Dover, Folkestone?'

'Garrison towns in peacetime, and we believe them to have considerable garrisons now. There would also be large numbers of naval personnel available for defence. And we have heard of a First London Division in the vicinity. But we have all the pre-war gun positions plotted – here . . . here . . . here.'

The major-general's anxious glances took note of the dubious way in which the colonel was pulling at his chin.

'What about these troops?' asked the colonel. 'Good? Bad?'

'Churchill boasted of bringing three hundred thousand men back from Dunkirk. But we have every scrap of equipment they took to France. They'll have rifles by now. Perhaps they'll have half their establishment of guns.'

'But they'll fight,' said the colonel.

'You captured Eben Emael,' the general replied. 'Can't you capture Dover Castle? Supposing you drop here, and here, on these Western Heights and on Edinburgh Hill, as they seem to be called. From there you could move down and seize the piers and the breakwater. The navy will have its ships alongside as soon as they are cleared and could land troops and armour by noon of the first day.'

The colonel hesitated longingly before he shook his head. 'Balloon barrages. In any case, we captured Eben Emael in time of peace,' he said. 'We can't hope for surprise this time. All those buildings will have garrisons and barbed wire. We have to fight our way through, yard by yard, five thousand men against ten thousand. The navy could do nothing until the harbour-defence guns were silenced, and they're the farthest out of reach. The odds are too heavy, general.'

The major-general nodded reluctant agreement. 'The navy won't be pleased to hear about your decisions,' he said. 'Nor will the general. They want a port.'

'The Tommies know that as well as we do. They'll be

strong there, and they'll be alert. We'll have to find a weak point and take it by surprise.'

'Yes,' agreed the general.

They stood looking at the map again.

'Now what about turning this flank?' suggested the colonel. 'That looks more promising.'

The colonel's pointer tapped its way over the map. 'Fairlight. Guestling. Udimore. Peasmarsh.'

'Houghton Green. Camber,' supplemented the general, warming to the scheme. 'Then you could isolate these places, Winchelsea, Rye.'

'I could clear a landing for the airborne troops *here*,' said the colonel. 'Then they can move in on this harbour – Rye Harbour. That might satisfy the navy.'

'There must be some landing facilities there.'

'There's twenty kilometres of beaches within that perimeter,' said the colonel.

He took a crayon from his pocket and with it marked a bold circle on each road radiating out from Rye and Winchelsea and then swept the crayon round in an arc, joining them from sea to sea.

'I wonder what the navy will have to say,' mused the general. He stood staring for several more seconds at that black line drawn so boldly on the map.

MUSSOLINI ENTERS THE WAR, said the headline. That was the clearest proof that France was finished as a military factor. Mussolini would never have ventured into the fighting unless he was sure that the war was almost over.

And that was the day that the fat and elderly barge captain put his wheel over and closed the throttle to allow the *Fritz Reuter* to turn into the river port on the lower Rhine. What he saw there as his barge went thump-thumping round the corner caused him to open his mouth with surprise. The port was filled with riverboats, more than he had ever seen at one time before in his life. Half the self-propelled barges of Germany – more than half, perhaps – were there, packed in, rank beside rank, and nearly all of them riding high in the water to prove that they were empty. There were friends and acquaintances everywhere, shouting greetings as soon as they recognised him and his barge.

'Well, we might have expected you!'

'You're a long way from home, aren't you, Hans?'

'The *Fritz Reuter*'s here, boys. Now war can start.'

The barge captain who shouted the last remark cut his words off short, with a note of apprehension in the final syllables, and he threw a frightened glance over his shoulder – the sort of glance which Germans had for years been casting behind them after a rash speech.

The remark had been natural enough, all the same. There was a gigantic battle being fought in France, and here was an unprecedented concentration of river shipping. There must be some connection between the two; but it might be as well not to comment on it.

Reynaud Cabinet Resigns; Marshal Petain Heads New Government, was the next headline. That meant not merely conquest, but an armistice. The new government would, as far as lay in its power, restrain Frenchmen all over the world from continuing hostilities.

It would simplify to some extent – to a minute extent – the problems confronting the colonel-general at the head of the conference table with the air general and the vice-admiral on either side of him and the half dozen other officers in descending order of rank further down the table.

'But you admit,' the colonel-general was saying to the vice-admiral – and those words were proof that accusation was being met by defence – 'you admit that the British managed to move three hundred thousand men across the Channel three weeks ago.'

The vice-admiral tried not to display impatience. 'Three hundred thousand men, sir, but not an ounce of equipment. And may I call the colonel-general's attention to the British Admiralty communiqué of June third? In that it is stated that two hundred and twenty-two naval vessels took part in the operation and six hundred and sixty-five other craft. And I hardly have to remind the colonel-general that the operation lasted a week.'

'And how many craft have you?'

'I hope to assemble nearly as many. Everything that floats. Every barge, every motorboat, every tug. The internal navigation of the Reich is at a standstill. Six weeks from now the consequences will begin to be deplorable.'

'Six weeks from now . . .' The colonel-general indulged in a moment's daydreaming before turning his gaze on the intelligence officer down the table. 'What have you to report?'

'Our best source of information is the English newspapers via Dublin. The British began to take urgent anti-invasion measures several weeks ago, and the parachute attack on Eben Emael and Rotterdam have hastened them. It is now forbidden to leave any motor vehicle unattended without first removing some necessary working part. Church bells are not to be rung except in case of invasion. There has been a general roundup of people suspected of favouring our cause, including some of our best friends.'

'But what about troops, man?'

'Not so easily discovered, sir. It appears obvious, I am afraid, that they have just brought back most of their First Armoured Division with their equipment. It may be back in its old area near Portland. There is a Second Armoured Division, not fully equipped nor trained, believed to be in the Lincolnshire area. There are about sixteen infantry divisions, including Canadians, in various stages of training, probably all short of artillery.'

'We shall be short of artillery as well, according to this scheme,' said the colonel-general, tapping the folder of typewritten sheets before him. 'What else?'

'The British have been for some time preparing a muster of all civilians in case of invasion. They are to assemble on the first alarm, armed with old rifles and shotguns and cavalry carbines. They are called the LDV – Local

152

Defence Volunteers.' The intelligence officer said these last three words in English and then added a German translation. There was an apologetic note in his voice – for wasting the colonel-general's time over such trifles.

'They might cause some loss to the parachute troops,' said the air general. 'If so . . .'

There appeared no need to finish the sentence.

HITLER STATES HIS TERMS, said the headline. But the very day the headline appeared, the terms were already agreed to. At Compiègne Hitler had his greatest hour. With the ceremony over Hitler strode out again. He halted by the monument with its inscription. Göebbels was there and handed him some typewritten sheets.

'The full translation of Churchill's speech of June eighteenth, *mein Führer*. There is a summary attached.'

Hitler flipped through the pages and called Göebbels' attention to a sentence. 'The whole fury and might of the enemy must very soon be turned on us.' Then there was another one. 'If the British Empire and its Commonwealth last for a thousand years, men will say, "This was their finest hour".'

'He will eat those words,' said Hitler.

It was only a subcommittee which sat considering the accumulated intelligence – half a dozen men, by no means of the highest rank – and yet the conclusions they were going to reach might affect all mankind through all subsequent history. In consequence they had to be men of steady nerve and yet men of imagination – nerve at the right moment and imagination at the right moment. It would not do to dwell too imaginatively on their responsibilities, to think about the colossal results of errors on their part. A single bad mistake, or a chain of minor ones, could mean that midsummer would see a triumphal march of panzers and Bersaglieri along the royal route from Buckingham Palace to the Mansion House; certainly that did not bear thinking about too much. But imagination had to be used; thousands of items of information had to be sifted and examined, and decisions reached as to whether they had any significance or not, and then further decisions as to how and by whom action should be taken.

This subcommittee was holding its meeting in one of the rooms in the war headquarters – one of the scores of rooms composing the labyrinth that stretched underground from Storey's Gate to Trafalgar Square, corridor below corridor, with the sewer pipes and water pipes and gas pipes of London twining through them amid a tangle of electric mains and telephone cables and air pipes. Dante could have fittingly described that war headquarters, from which the war could still have been conducted even if the city of eight million lay in ruins above it.

Inside this particular room the air-conditioning system struggled valiantly against the tobacco smoke that threatened to fill it. There were orderly banks of files against the walls; there were folders in plenty laid out upon the table round which the subcommittee was seated.

'Well, gentlemen,' said the chairman, 'it looks as if the pieces are fitting together.'

His rapid gaze shot round the table. Each pair of eyes met his in turn. There was something more than tobacco smoke in the air; there was a tension and an excitement even more noticeable.

'I shall need an appraisal to present to the War Cabinet this afternoon,' went on the chairman. 'That shouldn't be difficult.'

He glanced down at the chart of the English Channel that lay before him. On it were drawn two converging lines – the same two lines as had been drawn on a similar chart which had been discussed some time before by a German naval captain and a Luftwaffe colonel.

'These minefields which they persist in laying. They indicate an intention to seal off a section of the Channel for their own purposes. Yes? And the most likely purpose is invasion?'

'I can't think of any other reason,' said the naval member.

'And the German navy – the three big ships and most of the destroyers – is at Wilhelmshaven with all leave cancelled.'

'They might be planning a massed sortie into the Atlantic.'

'Or they might be intended to screen an invading force. Yes?'

'Yes,' said the naval member.

'Every barge in Germany,' went on the chairman, 'pretty nearly every one at least, is moving to the Channel coast by one route or another. Coal's already short in Berlin. Can that mean anything except invasion?'

'No,' said the naval member.

'Trawlers and minesweepers and tugs,' added the chairman. 'All moving down the Dutch coast. Invasion?'

'Certainly,' said the naval member.

'These air photographs. The Channel ports are full of barges already. Antwerp, Ostend, even Calais, and more waiting their turn. Any possible explanation except invasion?'

'None,' said the naval member.

The chairman picked up another folder. 'These army divisions. More than a dozen of them, with three or four good armoured ones among them. They made no appearance during the fighting in France. Why not?'

'A strategic reserve?' suggested the military member.

'Some of them marched directly away from the fighting. We have this one – the Eleventh – definitely located at Ostend. If you were Hitler, would you line up your strategic reserve along the Channel coast?'

'No,' said the military member.

'The Third Air Fleet took no part in the fighting either. It's been taking over the airfields in Holland and Belgium and Northern France.'

'That could mean anything,' said the air-force member. 'Sooner or later they're going to attack us.'

155

'But they'd be necessary there to give air cover for an invasion?'

'Oh yes, certainly.'

'These raids we've been having in the southern counties. Reconnaissance? Testing? Or just plain nuisance?'

'I wish I could be sure,' said the air-force member. 'But they'd do their best to conceal their object in any case.'

'But are they consistent with invasion plans?'

'They're not inconsistent, anyway,' said the air-force member cautiously.

'There's a parachute division and at least one air-landing division, and we've heard nothing from them since Rotterdam. Any comments?'

'There are enough planes to transport the whole para-chute division at a single drop – say six thousand infantry with mortars and a certain amount of equipment,' said the air member. 'The air-landing troops would have to follow, mostly. A few instantly and the rest in a second wave – three hours later, say.'

'Enough to be a nuisance.'

The chairman turned back to the naval member. 'How many can they transport by sea?'

'Depends entirely on how much equipment they bring with them. They might carry forty thousand infantry at one lift, to land on an open beach. Armour would reduce that number. But on the other hand, I wouldn't like the job of landing armour on an open beach. You want a port and quays and cranes for that, and *those* ports' – the naval member stabbed with his finger at the map – 'are not only defended but prepared for demolition in case of accidents.'

'Special landing craft?'

'A few experimental ones only. We'd have heard if they'd started building in large numbers.'

'So some armour might be landed?'

'No doubt. A division possibly, although it's hard to believe it.'

'Very well, gentlemen.' The chairman looked at the

clock. 'We are agreed that invasion can come at any moment.'

It was while the chairman was gathering his papers together – at that very same moment – that at the head-quarters at St Omer the chief of staff laid the final orders before the colonel-general for signature. The colonel-general turned the pages over with one hand while he held his fountain pen ready in the other. He scribbled his signature.

'The code word has gone out, sir,' said the chief of staff.

'Excellent,' said the colonel-general.

But he was enough of a romantic to spare a glance at the map on the table which was revealed when the chief of staff took the orders away. The road to London; there were strange foreign names upon it, Hawkhurst and Lamberhurst, Tonbridge and Sevenoaks – stepping stones on the road to victory, like Warsaw and Liege and Reims.

Motorcycle dispatch riders were already hurtling at speed over the roads of Holland and Belgium and northern France; they pulled up with a clatter, hurled themselves from their saddles to hand over their sealed envelopes to waiting officers. It took only a second for those officers to read the entire message inside – SEA LION. Sea Lion – Sea Lion – Sea Lion – on airfields and at ammunition depots, in railway stations and in field bakeries, in Calais, Brussels, Cologne, Berlin, those words were heard, and the Third Reich gathered itself for its boldest leap of all.

As darkness closed over the little harbours excitement mounted. Frenchmen and Belgians and Dutchmen, confined to their houses by a strict curfew, lifted their heads to hear, in each little port, a sudden tonk-tonk-tonking as the diesels started up in their hundreds. Mooring lines were cast off, and barges began to nose their way towards the entrances. There were misunderstandings and minor collisions. The orders that had until now been given in quiet executive tones were now being bellowed through megaphones, as if the officers concerned had suddenly realised that there was, after all, no danger of arousing England from her sleep across the water.

'Keep them moving! Keep them moving!' shouted the naval officer in charge of the embarkation into his telephone as the reports came in. It was his business to get as many loaded vessels out to sea as could possibly be managed while the tide served. No one knew better than he did the difficulties of the operation he was directing.

The fat captain of the *Fritz Reuter* spun his wheel urgently to avoid a dark shape looming in front of him. Beside him a young naval officer, no more than a boy, stared down at the faintly illuminated dial of a compass – a very new fitting in the *Fritz Reuter* – and stammered orders.

'Thank heavens!' said the young naval officer suddenly, the relief in his voice contrasting oddly with the apprehension in the fat captain's mind. 'There's the light. Follow it.'

It was the faintest red glow, shining back from the stern of an invisible motor gunboat. There were good navigators on board her, and she was detailed to show the way to as many self-propelled barges as could keep her light in sight. The two lectures that had been given to the young naval officer had laid stress on the difficulties of the crossing. It would take a long time to get all the vessels out of the crowded harbour, and during that time the tides of the Channel would sweep them eastward and then westward, scattering them in all directions if they did not cluster behind their allocated leaders. It might well happen that any of the young officers would find himself alone, responsible for his own navigation.

'In that case,' the German naval commander who had given the lectures added, 'no captain can be far wrong who lays his ship on the beaches of Dungeness.'

The *Fritz Reuter* went tonk-tonking over the quiet sea. It was a calm night, as the meteorologists had predicted. The little waves over which she wallowed and plunged were small for the Channel, although far larger than anything she had ever encountered before. The wind was no more than a gentle breeze from the southeast – nothing compared with the icy blizzards through which the fat captain had often steered the *Friz Reuter* along the Elbe and Havel.

A big harbour tug was following them; the captain of the *Fritz Reuter* could see her silhouette clearly, and faintly behind her he could see the barges she was towing – huge lighters strangely diverted from their usual business in Hamburg. A few minutes later he saw something else away out to starboard. He did not recognise it at first for what it was; it was only after the ship herself became visible that he realised that what had caught his attention was her white bow wave. She was coming along fast, running down-channel, picking her way through the myriad craft that dotted the surface of the water. She passed close astern of the *Fritz Reuter*, between her and the harbour tug, and the fat captain saw plainly the upper works and the guns that marked her as a fighting ship. There was another one following her closely behind.

'*Emden,* light cruiser,' said the young naval officer with a gulp of excitement, 'and that's *Nürnberg*.'

They passed as quickly as they had come; within a few seconds the *Fritz Reuter* was wallowing in quite terrifying fashion in the steep wash which they left behind them. The passing of those two ships gave an added quality of harsh reality to the strange, nightmare night.

Five minutes later they saw a sudden winking light appear ahead of them. It only endured for a second or two, and then they saw jets of red flame stabbing the darkness, and tiny pinpoints of flame replying from the point where the light had been seen.

There were red threads which the fat captain told himself were tracers, and a sudden burst of flame extinguished almost immediately, and then nothing, except for a second or two the sound of the firing still travelling back to them, in a higher key that made it audible to them over the

159

bass tonk-tonking of the diesels all round them.

It was several minutes later that they heard the cry, a loud call from the surface of the water.

'Keep on!' said the young naval officer.

The cry was repeated again and again, louder each time. Only fifty feet away, on the starboard bow, they could see who was calling; someone floating, probably in a life jacket.

'Keep on!' said the young naval officer, and they saw the dark spot on the sea pass astern of them, and they heard the cries gradually grow fainter.

For all his inexperience of war the fat captain could guess what had happened. Some tiny patrolling vessel out there had sighted the approaching flotilla, had challenged, and had been instantly overwhelmed by the fire of a motor gunboat or torpedo boat ahead. The fat captain, tense at the wheel, wondered how much of an alarm the enemy had been able to send off first, but he was interrupted in this train of thought by a new sound. At first it was almost inaudible among the muttering of the diesels, but the ear caught it plainer and plainer as it mounted in volume. It was the noise of aeroplane engines, by the hundred, by the thousand, louder and louder and louder, coming from astern, until overhead the din was deafening. Looking up, the fat captain was aware that the sky was already brighter, and against it he could see the planes faintly silhouetted, myriad flecks against the sky, racing over his head to the harsh music of that tremendous chorus, while the young naval officer capered with excitement, waving his arms as the things passed over them.

'Not long now,' he was saying, his young voice rising to an excited squeal.

The roar of those engines had been heard in many places. The civilians in Western Europe heard them go – the Luftwaffe. By the mere threat of its existence it had changed the course of history in peacetime. It was because of the Luftwaffe that the French and Belgians and Dutchmen, who had been free men less than two months ago, were now the helpless slaves of an irresponsible and reckless tyrant whose casual word could condemn them instantly to forced labour, hunger, or death. The tyrant had only one enemy left in the world; the civilians who heard the passing of the Luftwaffe could have no doubts as to where its blows were due to fall an hour hence. Few among them had any hope; despair was reaching deep into the hearts of all men on the European side of that strip of water.

Perhaps their children's children might win back to freedom; they felt that they themselves would die slaves.

On the far side of that strip of water were men who had never thought of losing hope. Some of them were gazing with unflagging attention into strangely illuminated screens, magical apparatus which could reveal danger as it advanced over the horizon. The machines themselves were still crude and comparatively insensitive; the men who sat by them were still inexperienced, almost untried in war. There were less than fifty machines; there were only a few hundred men responsible for their maintenance and handling. The impulses which actuated those machines were so infinitesimal that scientists of twenty years before would have laughed at the thought of their being of any practical importance whatever. Yet it was upon the proper interpretation of those infinitesimal impulses as received by those crude machines that the destiny of the world hinged.

Even then it seemed as if all the efforts of a thousand scientists and the planning of a thousand officers were directed towards a trivial object. Danger could be detected as it rose over a distant horizon, many, many miles away, but so rapidly would that danger approach that in twenty minutes it would be overhead. Twenty minutes from the first vague appearances on the screen. Twenty minutes for them to be noted and reported; for the right conclusions to be drawn from the reports; for decisions to be reached, based on those conclusions; for orders to be issued, based on those decisions; for those orders to be received and acted upon; for defenders to climb into the sky to meet the approaching danger. But that twenty minutes meant the difference between disaster and victory.

With those first appearances on the screens counter-measures began. Warning bells were pushed, voices spoke into mouthpieces. Drill and discipline left those voices steady and clear despite the surge of excitement in the breasts of the speakers.

Over the converging wires the messages began to stream into the Operations Room, between whose walls – as the designers had well known – the command would be exercised in the battles for the air. As the bearings were reported, symbols began to appear on the vast transparent map, put there by sober-faced men and moved in accordance with the new information as it came in. Senior officers stood to watch the chessboard on which they were about to play a game whose stakes were not such trivial matters as life and death, but slavery and freedom.

'It looks like everything they've got,' was the comment of one watchful officer to the other, as the reports flowed in of the immense air forces heading for England.

In the dark days of Munich, international relations had been dependent on one single factor – the thought of a massed attack by the Luftwaffe upon helpless cities. Imaginative people had tried to picture a rain of bombs falling on London, dropped by an air fleet of only vaguely known potentialities. It was that picture which had contributed to the ruin of Czechoslovakia, and which had caused the authorities in London to store up a hundred thousand cardboard coffins so that the sight of the dead being carried through the streets should not discourage the few still living. It was a long-standing tradition that the air war would begin by a massed attack of this sort. London might well be the principal point to be defended, and that seemed the more likely as it appeared certain that the Luftwaffe had put into the air every plane that could fly.

There could be no means of guessing that the objective of this enormous force was a tiny section along the sea of agricultural England, sheep pastures and shingles, ten miles long and five miles deep, containing no town of any importance and only an inconsiderable harbour.

The defending planes were standing by, with some few in the air, when the telephones began to ring and a flood of reports came pouring in to make it certain that the German eagle had swooped upon this minute objective at the farthest edge of the area to be defended.

This was a Sunday morning, the morning of June 30, 1940. It was the end of almost the shortest night in the year, and darkness was just beginning to give way before the very first hint of light. Plodding along the lane where the wild roses grew in the hedges was a group of a dozen men. They all wore the brassards of the Local Defence Volunteers, but only eight of them carried firearms. They were returning home after a night on duty, a night of discomfort, voluntary and unpaid – half a million men like them were at this moment doing the same. They stopped when they heard the distant roar of a thousand aeroplane engines, and peered tensely up into the sky. The roar grew louder – louder – louder, so it was no longer possible to hear the dawn chorus of the little birds all around them, even if the birds continued to sing in that frightful din. The sky overhead was still faintly pink with the dawn as the planes came over to darken it.

Then the sergeant, looking up, saw the air thick with specks, and then he saw the specks suddenly burst open, burgeoning out like flowers suspended in the air, hundreds of them. They would have been beautiful against the sky if an indifferent eye could have seen them.

'That's them, boys,' said the sergeant. 'They've come.'

Even the sergeant, an old soldier, stood transfixed for some seconds before he could act. The planes had swept away, and the parachutes, each with its dangling figure, were perceptibly nearer before he spoke again.

'You two,' he said. 'Run like the devil to the village. Get on the telephone. Wake up the postmaster and the bobby. And you two. Find old Stiles the verger and tell him to ring the bell. Ring the bell and go on ringing it. Come on, you others.'

He led them at a trot for a quarter of a mile before he pulled up and issued orders that spread them out along the bank. He slid one of his ten cartridges into the breech of his rifle and took aim. The first shot of the Battle of Britain echoed across the fields just as the church bells began to ring solemnly over the quiet countryside, bells here and bells there and soon bells everywhere, calling the country to arms against the invader. And telephones began to ring as well, and excited neutral correspondents ran wildly to telegraph offices.

The dawn that came up over New York five hours later saw newspapers for sale in the streets, each with a headline covering half the front page – ENGLAND INVADED! – and, as the day wore on, those headlines appeared in the streets of a thousand cities. ENGLAND INVADED!

II

From the moment the German parachute troops reached the ground, where Kent and Sussex join, the Battle of Britain exploded. At five o'clock on that Sunday morning the BBC was already broadcasting to a small audience; but so rapidly did the news spread that when the broadcast was repeated at 5.30 nearly all England was aroused and listening.

'German parachute troops,' said the disembodied voice, carefully free from any emotion whatever, 'have landed in the neighbourhood of Rye and Winchelsea. They are already being engaged by local troops. Meanwhile, attempts are being made to land considerable forces on the beaches of Dungeness and Winchelsea. Fighting is continuing by sea and air as well as by land. The public is requested to read the instructions issued on June eighteenth last regarding invasion. Fresh copies are already being posted up in public places. Remember the first rule

164

stated there. *"Stay put."* Remain where you are, do not panic, and stay put. And remember the last sentence of those instructions, "Think always of your country before you think of yourself." The prime minister will address the country later today at an hour which will be announced shortly.'

It was a fact on which Britain can always look back with pride – that there was no panic. There had been no denial as yet, and no disproof, of the multitudinous current stories about German parachutists dropping in Belgium and Holland disguised as nuns and bus conductors. The night before the invasion everyone in England believed these stories and was prepared to see saboteurs at every street corner, but this morning the British public behaved as paradoxically as it had when France fell. It heaved a sigh of something like relief and decided, *Now we can get down to business.* Anxious people sat by loudspeakers; a few thoughtless people tried to put telephone calls through to relations in the threatened areas, but the main embarrassment to the authorities arose merely from the rush of people to town halls or police stations asking how they could help. The Sunday workers went on with their jobs; fathers on their day off took the children out so as to leave mothers with a free hand. An American correspondent summed up the situation by saying, 'London appears to be less agitated than I expect Washington is at this moment'.

But the battle was being fought with the utmost fury by land and sea and air, and – as in every battle ever fought – the defenders met with reverses at the beginning as the concentrated weight of the attackers fell on the weak points. At Dover the four destroyers stationed there came steaming out, turning south-westward as they rounded the signal station on their way to attack the German troop transports. Anxious watchers on the cliffs at Folkestone saw them coming, steaming fast. But their speed did not save them from their first casualty. The watchers saw a

165

great fountain of water go up from the side of the last of the four and saw her lurch out of line, disabled and on the point of sinking. One torpedo from the salvos fired by the ambushed submarines, waiting for this very moment, had struck home. And worse was to come. The first the watchers saw of it was when a cluster of pillars of water rose up from the surface of sea close to the leader. It was then that they looked farther out, to see a dark shape rushing to intercept from where she had taken post during the night under the French shore.

'Pocket battleship,' said the destroyer captain with his eyes to his binoculars. 'Make this to the Admiralty. Have sighted –'

The sentence was not finished nor the signal sent, as an eleven-inch shell exploded under the bridge. Somebody took command of that destroyer and swung her round to the attack, limping after the other two. The 4.7's fired back, but even ten of those shells did not equal the destructive power of a single eleven-inch, and a moment later the *Lützow* brought her secondary armament into action as well. The destroyers were hit and hit again; the watchers saw smoke pouring from their hulls and streaming astern, and then the smoke began to rise more vertically as they lost speed, hiding the last act of the tragedy from the eyes of the watchers.

Momentarily at least the Reich had won command of the patch of sea over which the army had to be transported and supplied; later that day the British destroyers at the Nore, hastening to the attack, encountered even more formidable opponents in the battle cruisers *Scharnhorst* and *Gneisenau*, and were forced back. In the wider waters of the Channel to the west the mines freely sown and the massed U-boats and the two light cruisers Raeder had stationed there succeeded in the same way in holding back the light British forces hastening up the Channel.

In this desperate struggle Raeder had flung in every vessel that could float, risking – expecting – total loss if for a few days the barges and transports could cross and re-cross the Channel. Victory on land – the capitulation of England – would render negligible the loss of the German navy. The watchers on the cliffs witnessed other desperate battles, tiny skirmishes, but battles in which men died for their country, where drifters armed with Lewis machine guns fought yachts armed with rifles, where trawler fought trawler hand to hand by boarding, in that frantic struggle to stop or to maintain the traffic to the beaches at Camber.

There were troops to defend the coast where the parachutists struck, and they were not taken by surprise. They were already standing to when the first sound of the approaching air armada made itself heard; they were at their alarm posts and ready for action when the parachutists dropped. But they were only one battalion, and not up to full strength even so. With a thousand miles of vulnerable coast to defend, there could be no hope of posting strong forces everywhere; that battalion was only an outpost, with the usual outpost's duty of warning and delay. The warning went out, before the parachutists cut the wires, but the delay was pathetically short.

A single company held Camber, and that was assaulted at once by two of the three German battalions dropped inside the perimeter; it must be remembered that in this parachute attack the drops were far more successful than could usually be counted upon, closely spaced and without any intermingling of units. The survivors of the British infantry company later declared that 'not ten minutes' elapsed between the first alarm and the beginning of the assault – probably an underestimate. The company was outnumbered by five to one at least, and from the unexpected side – overland. The parachute troops were the cream of the German army, powerful young men, with officers selected for their energy and quickness of thought. The rapidity of their attack was astonishing, and within a few minutes they had reached the frail defences; the brief hand-to-hand struggle that ensued could have only one ending.

The handful of British prisoners had the mortification

of seeing, when the fighting had ended and they could take breath, the Camber beaches thick with German landing craft, and Rye Bay covered with other vessels coming in; it was a sight which held the attention even though far overhead the opening phase of that part of the Battle of Britain which was fought in the air was being fought out with a ferocity and determination unequalled in history.

The tiny garrison of Rye Harbour, on the other side of the Rother mouth, held out for some time longer; some of the victors at Camber were diverted to the attack there and, in fact, it was not until midday that the Martello tower was stormed. Rye itself stood no better chance. Four parachute battalions had been dropped on the four roads on the landward side of the town and, leaving small forces at road-blocks, they wasted no time before launching their converging attack. Already the first echelon of the air-landing division was being hustled out of its lanes beside the Winchelsea road where another parachute battalion awaited it, and it was this assault that sealed the fate of Rye. The dive bombers were attacking at the same moment, raining ruin on the town. The Germans burst into Rye from all sides, and the final struggle was fought out in the picturesque old streets, from house to house and from room to room over the wreckage left by the bombing.

Women cowering in the houses were unwilling witnesses, were pitiful victims. Desperate soldiers crouching beside windows ignored them as they peered out for shots at the German attackers creeping forward from corner to corner, and often a well-flung hand grenade left soldiers and women dead and dying on the floor together among the kitchen furniture.

The wave of attackers swept in over the little town like the tide over a rock. A ferocious final struggle ended in the storming of the Ypres tower, whose garrison died to a man in its defence; by ten o'clock in the morning the shattered town was quiet again, with the streets littered with dead, Germans and British, soldiers and civilians, women and men. There were only a few shots still to be heard, here and there, as the moppers-up hunted the last of the defenders down from the rooftops and out of the cellars. Winchelsea succumbed at much the same time – here horror was added to horror by the coincidence that no fewer than seven blazing aeroplanes, shot down from the skies above, came crashing within the narrow limits of the little village while the fighting was in progress.

The whole world was waiting for news, ever since the first announcement, waiting in agonised anxiety. Even in the opening days of the Battle of Belgium, when the Wehrmacht had its strength first really tested, the tension had not been in any way so acute. It was evening in Australia; it was still night in California. The fate of England was in the balance, and the world knew that its own fate was in the balance too. In Tokyo and in Madrid, Istanbul and Rio de Janeiro, people waited for news. Then it came, from Göebbels' organisation in Berlin.

'The forces of the Wehrmacht have landed in England. Progress is already rapid, and the German flag now waves in triumph over the cities of Rye and Winchelsea, two of the once-proud Cinque Ports. The prisoners taken are numerous and the German losses slight. The landing is proceeding satisfactorily. England, which for a thousand years has seen no foreign enemy on her shores, is tottering down to destruction.'

The Battle of Britain was fought in the air, on land, on the sea, and under the sea. In the feverish hours of that Sunday morning there was action at every point, and indeed it is to the credit of the German staffs that this was the case. In less than four weeks they made and executed plans whose flexibility and whose timing can only excite admiration. The first wave of German landing craft came into the beaches a half hour before high water, with the first light, only some minutes after the parachute troops touched ground and – almost incredibly – without a single casualty.

The *Fritz Reuter* was by no means loaded to her full draught, not nearly to the extent to which she was usually loaded when carrying cement to Berlin. Forty tons of her present cargo consisted merely of men, and men, even when no allowance is made for their comfort, make an awkward and bulky cargo to carry. The metal containers of supplies, particularly those filled with ammunition, were more congenial cargo, but even so they were bulky and space-wasting because of their limitation to thirty-seven kilograms – about eighty pounds – apiece. With four hundred men on board and eight hundred containers, the *Fritz Reuter* drew only four feet of water.

The fat captain was so distracted by the flight of the Luftwaffe overhead that he actually had not noticed the low shore ahead. In the faint light he could just see, when the naval officer excitedly pointed to it, the line of small breakers, the beach and the low sandhills ahead. He swung his wheel over so as to come in squarely; all around him other craft were racing at their ponderous fastest for the same objective. The fat captain eased his throttle, but the beach was far shallower than he expected, and the *Fritz Reuter* took the ground with a bump that threw the excited soldiers in heaps. But there was an active major in command, who hauled himself up on deck again at once and bellowed orders. The men moved forward in orderly fashion into the bow and climbed up and leaped down into four feet of water. One platoon waded to the water's edge and pressed forward to the dunes to guard against an attack that was never made. The others formed two parties, one hauling forward the containers and handing them down to the other.

As fast as the containers were handed down the men in the water carried them up and dumped them at high-tide mark and returned again for the rest. The *Fritz Reuter* rose with the removal of her cargo as well as with the rising of the last of the tide; the fat captain had to let in the clutch at intervals to keep her bow aground so that the later journeys were far shorter than the first. It seemed hardly any time before the barge was free of its cargo, and the major waved farewell before he leaped down into the water on the heels of his men. In obedience to the young naval officer's order the fat captain engaged his reverse, and the *Fritz Reuter* drew off the beach, swung round and headed back towards France.

It had been unbelievably simple; the fat captain could hardly believe that his mission was accomplished. But he was so engrossed with the business of handling the *Fritz Reuter* that he had had eyes for little else — for the numerous boats that had not succeeded at all in getting their cargoes ashore, for the confusion and the accidents all around him. Overhead a chaotic din of engines and gunfire heralded the beginning of an air battle; he had been awake all night and was stupid with want of sleep. He could not think at all while the *Fritz Reuter*, empty now, plunged and flapped on the waves.

At Fighter Command Headquarters the situation revealed itself with instant clarity. It was as if a curtain had risen so that now the stage with its cast and its scenery was suddenly disclosed, fully lighted, to a waiting audience. One moment everything was uncertainty, and the next there could be no doubts at all.

A thousand planes in the air might have meant anything, and then the reports poured in, from the Observer Corps and the army, from the Local Defence Volunteers and the navy. Parachute troops and dive bombers; the Channel covered with shipping; the whole German plan was plain instantly, without any doubt at all. The attack from Stavanger upon the east coast, which the Luftwaffe intended as a powerful distraction, could not divert attention from their real objective for a moment. Fighter Command sent its squadrons speeding over the southern counties to deal with the invaders, leaving a minimum force to meet the eastern attack – and incidentally to gain one of the most striking victories in the war. The surprise which the Germans had sprung gained them only a few minutes of immunity – valuable minutes, but no more than that.

The Luftwaffe had planned as carefully as they could, drawing upon the experience gained in a hundred recent battles in which they had given air support to the ground troops, but the problems they faced here were hard of solution. It was a turning of the tables; a month ago the RAF had struggled to provide air cover at Dunkirk, over a distant beach against enemies with bases near at hand; today the Luftwaffe was trying to do the same thing at Rye Bay. They could put fighter squadrons in the air over the invasion area, but the time they could stay there was limited and was greatly reduced by the need to fly from France and to return. Against them was ranged an enemy who could mass his forces for an attack at his selected moment, and who enjoyed at the same time the advantage of radar to make the selection of that moment all the easier.

For the first twenty minutes of the air war the Luftwaffe had had the advantage of surprise, and had made the utmost use of it. The parachute troops had been dropped, a fair proportion of the air-landing troops had reached ground, and the dive bombers had begun their fearful and accurate attack upon Winchelsea and Rye. Then the picture changed like a dissolving view, and it never was to change back again. The Spitfires and the Hurricanes came in to the attack, the squadrons roaring in across the southern counties in obedience to the radio orders. There were fighters to meet them – Messerschmitts waiting high in the sky to protect their charges, but only a limited number, for the Germans' Third Air Fleet had to plan to have Messerschmitts in the air over there all day long.

While the battle was being fought in the upper strata, the slaughter took place in the lower – when two squadrons of Spitfires got in among the dive bombers and the troop-carrying planes. The Junkers 87s stood no chance against them at all; for a few wild minutes shattered and blazing wrecks rained down out of the sky into the sea, and into Sussex and Kent. The troop carriers were more vulnerable still. The latecomers of the first wave and the leaders of the second wave alike succumbed. German soldiers loaded down with weapons, squatting stolidly in the planes winging their way to the invasion coast, had mercifully only a few seconds in which to anticipate their fates. Squatting there, deafened and stupefied by the roar of the engines, their only warning came when bullets ripped through the fuselage, killing a few, wounding a few, before pilots and engines alike were struck dead by a concentrated burst. Then the plane rolled over and crashed to the earth, where death awaited the wounded and the unwounded.

The initial planned timing of the Luftwaffe had been perfect, as was only to be expected of that force with its very considerable experience. The parachute drop, the beginning of the air landing, the bombing of Rye and Winchelsea, and the intervention of the first escort fighters had taken place at the exact moments of greatest effect. But as the morning wore on, the standard could not be maintained. Keen minds at Fighter Command were watching the developments, and the reports came in more and more smoothly as the staffs settled down to their work. Cool calculations revealed the selected moment; one force of German fighters on its way back to France to refuel and rearm, another heading for England, but only just making its appearance on the screens, and a very limited force over the invasion area. That was the instant to seize the opportunity, to send the Spitfires and the Hurricanes roaring into action to strike at the Messerschmitts with odds of more than two to one, nearly three to one. Ten minutes of wild fighting almost emptied the sky of German planes, and after the second of these battles there was a moment when Bomber Command could intervene, to roar over the beaches raining explosives on the huddled shipping, on the crowded men and the dumped supplies.

Those keen minds at Fighter Command – and the keen mind at Downing Street – watched with anxiety the rising figures of reported losses, British and German. The RAF had had a month in which to recover from the wounds inflicted at Dunkirk, a fortnight in which to recover from those inflicted in France, long enough to complete the training of a considerable number of pilots; while for six weeks now the factories had exceeded all previous records of production. Reserves were scanty, but on the other hand the Luftwaffe had not recovered from its efforts in France either. The total of shattered British planes rose steadily; the total of dead and disabled pilots rose more slowly, with the recovery of many unwounded pilots. Even allowing for duplication and for error, it was becoming apparent that the balance was heavily in favour of the British; the German losses were close to, if not over, that figure of double the British losses which meant that in this deadly game of beggar-my-neighbour the Luftwaffe would be beggared first.

'Nothing new? No surprises?' asked the voice on the telephone.

'No, sir, nothing new,' was the reply from Fighter Command.

There had always been the lurking fear that when Hitler struck his blow he would employ some new weapon, some unexpected technique, but it was becoming clear that there was no new weapon in his armoury. Dive bombing, air landing, parachutists – all these were familiar already; it was comforting to know that some new defence had not to be hurriedly improvised against some new form of attack.

At eleven in the morning the Luftwaffe staff attempted what some among them had believed beforehand to be a masterstroke. They launched a fleet of bombers with fighter escort against London, in the hope both of finding a weak spot in the defences and of confusing the general issue. That was the first of the bad raids on London; five hundred tons of explosives killed a thousand civilians, laid streets in ruins, called forth the utmost efforts of the rescue and fire-fighting parties, but hardly forwarded the invasion in the least; German experts later believed that the same attack directed against roads and railways leading to the invasion area would have brought more decisive results, but that is doubtful to say the least. In any case the cost to the Luftwaffe – for the RAF inevitably attacked the raiders before they could escape – was very considerable, while the necessity of escorting the bombers left the invasion area almost unguarded.

The radio announcement of the invasion had appealed to the British public to 'Stay put', and it was notable how this instruction was obeyed by all sections of the community – save one. The Local Defence Volunteers for fifty miles around, and farther, without orders and without organisation, spontaneously went into action, the first in the field with a unanimity that astonished neutral observers out of touch with British feeling. In hundreds of villages and towns, in thousands and thousands of cottages and semi-detached dwellings, the volunteers kissed their wives good-bye and went off to the scene of action with their rifles – such as had rifles – and a pocketful of ammunition, if they had any. The nearest came on foot, the more distant on bicycles – within an hour of the first alarm the Hastings road and all the others leading from Maidstone and Chatham and Ashford and Guildford were crowded with cyclists pedalling on, ignoring the efforts of police and military police.

The later arrivals served to swell the forces already gathered about the focal points on the dozen roads radiating out from Winchelsea and Rye. Here there was German infantry, fierce, hard men who had seized farmhouses and cottages, driving the women and the old men out across the fields. They had set up their strong points, and they had posted their machine guns sheltered in ditches

175

and behind banks with a good field of fire, establishing themselves in a perimeter to guard the invasion area from attack. Round the perimeter gathered the clouds of volunteers, under no general command, most of them in groups of twenty or so led by sergeants or self-appointed leaders.

There were many rash groups and individuals – some of them mere sightseers – who exposed themselves and were mowed down by bursts of machine-gun fire. There were plenty whose curiosity was easily satisfied or whose courage evaporated and who drifted homeward as evening approached, but many remained, and among them were individuals, and groups commanded by individuals, with their fighting instincts aroused. There were two foolish attacks at Udimore, there was at least one at Peasmarsh, when madness overcame the huddled masses and they rose to their feet and went forward, yelling, to be mowed down in rows leaving heaps of pathetic corpses in the fields.

There were other individuals and groups better trained or more intelligent. They came creeping along the hedges, filtering through the copses, crawling along ditches. Many a German infantryman, peering forward to guard against an attack from the front, died from a bullet fired from behind him. The higher country, along which ran the roads, was so broken up with orchards and woods that it was not difficult for a determined man to make his way through the slender cordon of German troops. In the flats there were ditches and drains; a man who did not mind getting wet could crawl along those for miles, literally, screened by reeds. The men who did so were not the type who would waste ammunition, especially with no more, usually, than ten cartridges. There were targets in plenty within the perimeter, where the Germans were toiling to assemble their forces. It was easy from a bank of reeds to send a bullet winging into a working party of a battalion forming up – a smoothbore bullet, often enough, for a week ago there had been the first issue of bullet-loaded cartridges to fit a twelve-gauge shotgun; big bullets that could kill a man at two hundred yards. So while the battle was being fought overhead in the air and out at sea, it was being waged on land by these guerrilla troops.

By late afternoon in England it was still only midday in New York, where an eminent commentator was trying to explain the situation to a radio audience.

'The world is holding its breath awaiting the result of this battle,' he said. 'Everything depends upon it – the continued existence of Britain as a nation, the fate of Europe and, I need hardly tell you, the future of the United States as well. It appears as if the Germans have been fantastically fortunate in being able to slip a considerable force across the Channel, although that has always been considered possible. How big that force is and of what it is composed, we do not know, and nobody is likely to tell us. What we do know is that the Germans have not succeeded yet in seizing a harbour of any importance. Rye Harbour is only a tiny place, fit for only the smallest vessels to use, and it dries out at low water. It can contribute almost nothing to the maintenance of the invaders. Supplies and reinforcements will have to be landed on open beaches in so far as they are not brought by air.

'The Royal Navy may have been caught napping – we don't know – but I think we can safely say that they will soon cut off all means of supply by sea unless the Luftwaffe is able to keep them away. Meanwhile the Luftwaffe and the RAF are fighting desperately for the command of the air. We hear of continuous fighting in the air over the invasion areas. Berlin is claiming victories, but so are the British communiqués in a more quiet way. Everything may hinge on the results of the air fighting.

'The one solid fact that we do know is that a German army is established on the soil of England, fewer than sixty miles from London. Last month the German armoured columns broke through the combined British and French armies and poured across France. One week after they began their attack they were in Paris – and Paris was much farther away from the front than London is now.

Perhaps at this time tomorrow, when I speak to you again, I shall have to tell you that London has fallen. It is a solemn thought.'

The commentator ended his talk at this point, and then five seconds later he was on the air again.

'Here is a message that has just been handed to me. A German armoured column has entered the village of Northiam, about fifty miles from London. Fighting is continuing.'

The German invasion fleet was composed of 'everything that could float' – riverboats and lighters, motorboats and tank barges. It had been a remarkable feat on the part of the German naval command to assemble all these craft in the limited time allowed. It was a very mixed flotilla, and almost none of it was adapted for the purpose; during all the turbulent years of Nazi rule no plans at all had been made for the invasion of England, and nothing had been done to provide shipping for the purpose.

The most valuable part of the whole vast fleet were the twenty experimental landing craft, which the German navy had built some years ago with an eye to possible amphibious operations in the Baltic. If there had been two thousand of them rather than twenty, the German problems would have been simplified; but there were not. On the other hand, if those twenty landing craft had not been in existence, the Germans might as well not have made the attempt at all. Eighteen of them succeeded in making the crossing, beached themselves, dropped their ramps and disgorged their armour, sending a respectable squadron of tanks waddling up the shingle of the beach under the despairing eyes of the last of the British garrison making their last stand in the Ypres tower.

The dozen experimental amphibious tanks sent at the same time – all there were – were not so successful, five of them foundering when launched. But the young and active German general, looking about him as his command car carried him out of the landing craft and up to the road to the Golf Club House, was at that moment much encouraged. Ahead of him the firing had ended with the storming of Camber; behind him the beaches were thick with vessels disgorging men and cargoes. The sight filled him with hope; it might have filled a British onlooker with despair.

But a closer look, a more understanding appraisal, might lessen the hope and temper the despair. The *Fritz Reuter* had landed four hundred men with food and ammunition and had got away again in half an hour, but she was exceptional. A big river barge can be laden with artillery, can be run across a narrow arm of the sea, and can be beached on the far side in four feet of water, but what happens next? How to get the guns out and up on to firm land? There were no cranes to heave up the five-ton monsters, no ramps to haul them along, even when the ebbing tide left the barges dry on firm sand.

The German staffs had foreseen these difficulties, but it was not so easy to remedy them. German engineers with small explosive charges set to work blowing off the bows and blowing open the sides of the barges – a heroic remedy indeed. Then the guns could be hauled out on to the sand, to sink axle-deep, and the weighty ammunition cases dumped beside them, under the warm sun of that Sunday morning. But there were more than a hundred craft which had not succeeded in beaching themselves properly. They had taken the ground at an angle, had found an uneven patch of beach, and they rolled over with the receding tide, helplessly, their cargoes tumbling down, crashing through decks and hulls in confusion and ruin.

There were barges full of horses – it is very hard to realise at this late date, that the German army in 1940 was largely horse drawn – and when those horses had been coaxed on to the beach, fodder had to be found for them, and water; water above all, thousands and thousands of gallons of fresh water. Horses in this first wave of invasion had been kept to a minimum, but the half-tracks and the light armoured cars and the troop-carrying trucks were, if

179

anything, more difficult to get on to the beach, and for them petrol would be needed soon; the full tank trucks were the most obstinate vehicles of all to disembark, while hoses had to be run from the beached tank barges up to firm ground.

What complicated all these operations was the confusion of the landing. The German navy had done its best to minimise the confusion, but they had not achieved a great deal in face of all the handicaps. The need to use widely separated small harbours, the mixing of the flotilla by the tides, the unsuitable craft that had to be employed, the small tonnage available, all conspired to create muddle. The advance echelons of no fewer than four infantry divisions and two armoured divisions had reached the beaches, but in no order at all.

The close-packed rank of beached craft extended for ten miles, from Pett Level almost to Dungeness; and men and vehicles, guns and generals, supplies and spares, were scattered from end to end of this line; the German navy had had to accept this muddle because they could not contemplate for one moment any plan to sort out the invasion fleet in sight of land; that would have taken hours if it could have been done at all. So from right to left and left to right huddles of men were seeking their battalions, and colonels ran about under the hot sun trying to assemble their regiments. Generals shouted themselves hoarse – one at least died of heart failure hurrying over the sand dunes – and through the confusion half-tracks ploughed their way, seeking their guns, and frightened horses galloped whinnying, while overhead raged the air battle.

It was into this confusion that Britain's Bomber Command struck in the intervals when the Luftwaffe could not maintain air cover over the beaches. They dropped their bombs like beads on a string along the crowded strip. The damage done was not overwhelmingly severe nor the casualties oppressively great, but the confusion and demoralisation were enormous when the half-assembled battalions dispersed for cover all over the flats; it was as well for the landing force that the third bombing raid devoted itself to the seagoing vessels anchored out in Rye Bay trying to hoist out their cargoes; those were easy targets, and not a single ship escaped.

Quite early in the day the first bullets fired by the LDV began to be noticed. There were not many of the volunteers skilful enough, or devoted enough, to make their way, after penetrating the paratroop cordon, within range of the beaches, by ditch and gorse clump; two or three hundred perhaps in all, but they played a useful part. A colonel standing, trying to get his regiment formed up, would break off in the middle of a word and fall dead to the ground; a group of men hastening along the track would hear a shot in the distance and would see one of their comrades tumble down with a shattered thigh. So harassing were these continual losses that the first-formed troops had to be dispersed again at once and sent out to scour the flats. They accomplished the task in great part – many unknown Englishmen died that afternoon – but at the cost of being unavailable for unloading, and they fired off thousands of cartridges, and every cartridge on this side of the Channel was worth a thousand, a hundred thousand, over in France.

In London, telephones were ringing, orders were being sent out, reports coming in.

'Isn't your division on the road by now? Report in half an hour that it's moving, or someone else will be in command.'

'What's the latest from the First London?'

'Send this order to Montgomery ...'

The central government, volcanic in its energy thanks to its prime minister, was moving every available man concentrically against the invasion area. Inexperienced staff officers were tackling the task of pulling a division out of London and hurrying it south.

'Is there any chance of this being just a feint, and the

real landing somewhere else?' asked a cautious voice.

'None at all,' was the prompt reply; the prime minister had gauged accurately enough the limits of the capacity of the German air force and navy. 'No need for more than a battalion in Dover and Folkestone now. The rest of that division ought to be moving to the attack.'

'Are those trains assembled yet? The first one should leave by noon.'

'Has the Fleet cleared Scapa?'

'What are the last figures from Fighter Command?'

'Roadblocks are all very well, but I won't have the movement of our troops hindered.'

Until the actual eve of the invasion the staff responsible for the defence of England had held to the opinion that the German attack, if it came at all, would be launched against the east coast; the difficulties of the long sea passage had been underestimated and the advantages of the Lincolnshire area for armoured movement had been given too much weight. It was in Lincolnshire that the Second Armoured Division was stationed, and it was to the north of the Thames that the greater part of the ready divisions were distributed. But England is a small country, and it is covered with a network of railways accustomed, on such occasions as bank holidays, to transporting as many people as would outnumber a dozen divisions. There was enough rolling stock available for any conceivable effort, and to supplement the work of the railways there were large fleets of buses. The means to effect a rapid concentration were there; what was needed besides were the drive to bring it about and the staff to work to make it possible. There were some incredible blunders made – fantastic to look back on today – but the civilian railway authorities were on hand to correct most of them. And there was no lack of drive; that need hardly be said, considering who was at the head of the government. By noon on that Sunday, British forces were rolling forward everywhere in England to the attack.

The quality of those forces was another question entirely. The loss of the whole of the equipment of the Expeditionary Force at Dunkirk had almost disarmed the army. There were divisions which could not be considered as fighting forces at all; they had never exercised as divisions – indeed had never been formed up in one place – their artillery amounted to a single battery each of obsolete guns, and their transport simply did not exist, so that if they set out on a march it was doubtful if the men could be provided with a daily meal. It was a remarkable achievement to the credit of the division in garrison in East Kent – the luckless battalion annihilated at Winchelsea and Rye was a part of this – that it managed to get itself on the move westward at all. Using trains and buses and marching on foot, it pushed forward two weak brigades to New Romney and Appledore and patrols from there to make contact with the parachute troops. They had four field guns between them, and they were dependent for their communications on tradesmen's delivery vans commandeered in Folkestone and Dover.

On the other side the small garrison of Hastings had not so far to go to gain contact with the enemy. A short march up the road through Ore found them exchanging shots with the parachute battalions at Fairlight and Guestling. Mothers in their houses saw soldiers abruptly entering and heard the brief words 'Better get out, ma, while you can.' Evening services in churches were interrupted – and terminated – by the entrance of clattering platoons. Inexperienced subalterns under the direction of hardly more experienced engineer officers set about the task of turning cottages into strongpoints, heaving the poor sticks of furniture to one side, digging up the rich mould of the flower beds to fill sandbags, fortifying themselves in roadblocks that would at least delay the movement of the invaders; while all the time, it must be remembered, the air battle went on overhead, sometimes dying down, sometimes flaring up, but never quite lulled.

The blue sky above was streaked everywhere with the white condensation trails of a thousand planes, and often a soldier would raise his eyes from his task of filling sand-bags or a volunteer would spare a moment from his watch over a hedgerow to see a plane come hurtling down out of the upper blue, trailing smoke behind it, to plunge into the fields with a shattering crash.

'There goes another. Can't be many left by now.'

The British soldier never doubted that these were all German planes crashing down.

There was in England on this Sunday, June thirtieth, one hundred and thirty heavy tanks all told, no more. And even that number represented a great increase on the figure after Dunkirk, when there were hardly more than seventy. These were the lumbering old I tanks, but highly efficient fighting machines by the standards of 1940. There were, on the other hand, more than five hundred light tanks. Most of this armour was distributed over two armoured divisions, the First in Dorset – a war-hardened force with experience in France – and the Second in Lincolnshire, and these two divisions were the principal concern of the railways, moving them ponderously to interpose them between the invaders and London. There was no certain knowledge as yet of how great a force had landed, but every British pilot returning from a sweep over the invasion area could report having seen the squat, fore-shortened shapes of German tanks moving along the roads and lanes beside Winchelsea and Rye.

German tanks! The word reached headquarters speedily enough. What was there to stop them if they came raging up the roads to London?

In war there is always the likelihood of attributing to the enemy strength and mobility and knowledge quite beyond reality. It was in the fear that German tanks might appear in the suburbs that very afternoon that the precautions were hurried on. Explosives were taken from every storage depot and hurried by car and truck along the Surrey roads, where Royal Engineers, whirled by car from their billets, set about preparing the bridges for demolition. The LDV toiled to create roadblocks; it was actually no later than four o'clock in the afternoon that the first 'sticky bombs', made by hand in frantic haste in London factories, were being issued to LDV on the main roads. A devoted man, with the greatest good fortune, could perhaps cripple a tank with one of these – might even conceivably destroy it, at the cost of his life. There were dozens of men who took those 'sticky bombs' in hand in the fixed but almost wordless intention of giving their lives to help to stop the German armour.

Guns would stop armour if given a chance; there were five hundred field guns in the whole of England, mostly scattered in single batteries here and there among scores of units, mostly manned by half-trained artillerymen. But some were attached to the divisions brought back from Dunkirk, to which more could be sent. A day or two would see those divisions, fully trained and half-equipped, rolling forward to attack the invaders. Meanwhile?

Meanwhile a few batteries could be dug in to cover the roads leading into London, and supported by packets of battalions painfully made mobile, while an ex-cavalry officer with a cigar chafed at the delay and demanded an instant offensive, and women and children stood in the sunlit streets and lanes to watch the buses packed with soldiers rolling by.

III

The *Führer* at his headquarters was chafing no less. He knew what there was at stake. Habitual gambler though he was, he could not keep calm while the dice was still rolling, while he waited for the enemy to show his hand. The first reports had brought elation, but the ones that followed brought first irritation and then anger. By good management the parachute troops had landed; by a miracle of good fortune the invasion flotilla had reached the beaches; by a combination of management and luck there was a squadron of tanks ready for action on British soil; by hard fighting Winchelsea and Rye were in German hands. But then the Luftwaffe began to straggle back to the airfields to rearm and refuel – and to count their losses.

At first Goering handed the figures over to his chief without checking them, but the explosion of wrath and the cutting sarcasm which they provoked made him more cautious. After that he edited the figures. He began to allow ten per cent for planes descending at other than their own airfields; he omitted all mention of the damaged planes which had crawled home and would not fly again for days or weeks; to be on the safe side he added ten per cent to the estimated British loss, even though that could not be checked and was certainly overestimated already. Then he could show figures that at least made optimism possible.

Now the headquarters signal station was set up at Rye Harbour and the first weak messages from England could be supplemented by later ones, clear and strong, but yet conveying only a faint picture of the disorder on the beach.

No complete unit had yet formed. Unloading was beginning.

'Beginning? Are they asleep over there?'

Civilian snipers were causing loss.

'Civilians? What is he thinking about? Order him to take the strongest measures. Shoot them. Hang them. Take twenty – fifty – a hundred of them and hang them from trees. This village here – Guestling Green – tell him to burn it and teach them the laws of war.'

Enemy infantry patrols had appeared at – The message ended there abruptly, and there followed a long silence, ominous as well as infuriating, before communication was resumed by a weak transmitter. The beaches had been bombed for the fourth time. Headquarters had been hit, the general was dying of his wounds, the whole command apparatus shattered.

'That's a disgrace. Where was our fighter cover? Goering, you must do better than this. See that there is fighter cover continuously over the beaches.'

'Very well, *mein Führer*.'

Goering, who falsified figures, was not the man to point out that this *Führer* Order was impossible to obey, and dreadfully expensive to attempt to obey.

'You, General. Cross at once and take command. Put some life into them.'

'Very well, *mein Führer*.'

The weak transmitter was still sending messages. Every ship in the bay had been bombed and sunk at anchor, and the *Führer* turned an angry glance at his naval commander-in-chief.

'*Mein Führer*, I have already stated in writing that a landing by sea was a dangerous operation without complete control of the air. When darkness comes I have ships ready to try again.'

'And what about this confusion on the beaches?'

'*Mein Führer*, I have stated in writing also that it was impossible with the means available to land a force in instant readiness to fight.'

The naval commander-in-chief had up to now been in high favour not only on account of his remarkable success in landing the army but also because of that morning's successful battle with the British destroyers off Folkestone. But now a string of reports were coming in which were not so favourable. The British Fleet had been sighted coming south – an aircraft carrier, battleships, cruisers and destroyer screen. With the Fleet moving fast and heavily screened, the U-boats were attacking in vain. The massed onslaught planned for the Fleet's exit from Scapa had failed, not unnaturally; the British admiral, called forth by the news of invasion, could expect nothing else and was doubly on his guard. Seven U-boats had made the attempt, and now only one was reporting.

'Is Lütjens ready for them?'

'Yes, *mein Führer*. He will fight to the death.'

'Tell him every hour he delays them is precious.'

'Yes, *mein Führer*.'

'Have you given orders to bomb them, Goering?'

'Not as yet.'

'Then why do you wait for me to tell you? Give the orders at once.'

'Yes, *mein Führer.*'

It was easy enough to say 'yes', but not so easy to carry out the promise. Goering's forces were at full stretch already. But Goering was Goering, who would never admit that anything was beyond the powers of the Luftwaffe, and he said, 'Yes, *mein Führer.*' The mere effort of trying to maintain fighter cover over the invasion beaches while the transport planes dropped supplies was something a trifle beyond the Luftwaffe's strength, but here was Goering launching air raids on London and diversions from Norway and endeavouring to play a part in the naval fighting in the North Sea and in the Channel all at the same time.

The dashing young general commanding the armour on the invasion beaches was already fretting and champing at the bit. He had forty heavy tanks at his disposal now, armed and fuelled and ready to march, and London was no more than two long marches away from where he waited at Playden, his tanks distributed through the village, while the battle in the air still raged above him. But even forty heavy tanks were not sufficient for a decisive blow. Between him and London there was infantry, he knew; there would be roadblocks, there were a few guns, possibly. He needed artillery to help him on his way and motorised infantry to follow him up; he needed bridging equipment and air reconnaissance, and none of this was available as yet. Moreover, he had only to look behind him, down the hill from Playden, to see a huge column of smoke mounting up into the blue sky from the beaches; the last bombing attack there had hit two of his invaluable tank barges, and that smoke was rising from a million gallons of petrol pouring in blazing rivers down into the sea. He drummed with his fingers as he sat high up in his

188

command car in the shadow of Playden church.

That was when the old gentleman came along, the colonel, who had first been under fire in the Boer War and who had survived three wounds at Arras and the Somme. He was the only civilian in sight; such of the other inhabitants of Playden who had not fled before the parachutists were sitting apprehensively in cellars and kitchens. But the colonel walked boldly along. The empty sleeve showed that he was only a crippled noncombatant; his remaining hand was in the side pocket of his tweed coat. And running through his mind was Churchill's phrase, 'You can always take one with you'.

The keen blue eyes recognised the command car and the general with the Iron Cross under his chin. The old Mauser pistol, which had been his mascot on the Somme, had three rounds still in the magazine – thirty years old, but when he pulled out the pistol and pressed the trigger, they did their work. The young general fell headlong out of the command car, tumbling to the road with a look of surprise still on his face, and the colonel fell four yards away from him, riddled by bursts from the pistols of the general's infuriated staff.

So when Von Rundstedt climbed out of the Storch plane that put him down beside the Rye road, the first news that greeted him was that the general commanding his armour was dead – a piece of news almost as depressing as the sight of the confusion on the beaches and the smouldering wrecks of planes that littered the fields wherever he looked. Those fields were patched like Joseph's coat in many colours, when ten thousand parachutes lay scattered over them; and among the parachutes and the smoking wrecks and the guerrillas creeping from one cover to another there were still the sheep grazing industriously and lifting their noses to baa to their half-grown lambs.

The divisional general commanding the parachute troops made his report to Von Rundstedt. British armoured cars had made their appearance at Beckley, exchanging shots with the battalion there; the guerrilla troops were harassing the perimeter at all points from the sea round to the sea again. A single order from Von Rundstedt was sufficient to send the armour rolling forward under a new general. The people of Playden heard the engines roar and heard the ponderous clank of the armour getting under way. Up the road they rolled in a monstrous column, probing forward towards London, clanking in their mechanised might through Peasmarsh and bursting out of the perimeter at Four Oaks and at Beckley. The Local Defence Volunteers strung along ditches and hedges saw the monsters charging down at them by lane and field, and their bullets rang impotently against their steel sides. Some of the volunteers died, some ran for their lives, and some few, crouching in coppices, let the wave roll by and waited on in ambush for more vulnerable targets. In Northiam they fought to the death, holding their pitifully incomplete defence works as the armour came pouring in from all sides into the village. The 'sticky bombs' had not been delivered here yet; the few hastily contrived anti-tank weapons – bottles of petrol – were ineffective, although some unknown good soldier set fire to the small amounts of petrol at the filling stations, thus keeping it out of the hands of the Germans. The German armour suffered no loss at all, but at Bodiam and Newenden and Udiam men working furiously with picks and shovels, and helped at the last moment by engineer detachments arriving by car with explosives, destroyed the bridges over the Rother. Von Rundstedt had pushed out his perimeter by half a dozen miles; he had dealt a severe blow to the morale of the Local Defence Volunteers in this sector, and he had provided a line for a bulletin, but he had done no more.

And meanwhile by road and by railway the British army was slowly moving forward to the point of danger. Forty trains could transport a division, and there were a thousand trains available, chugging along branch lines and thumping over points at obscure junctions as trains took unprecedented routes from north to south and from west to east, as Montgomery gathered the Second Corps together to move in from Hampshire and the Second Armoured circled London on its way from Lincolnshire.

And the Fleet was steaming south from Scapa, picking its way through the minefields; and from the west a hastily gathered force of cruisers and destroyers was already moving up the Channel to make an abrupt end of the momentary German command of the sea there.

Yet in a sense none of this was as important as the air battle which was still raging over the invasion area. It was here that the vital decision would be reached, and victory would be owed – if victory were to be won – to the few hundred fighter pilots at the disposal of the RAF. It could be argued that Hitler would have done better for himself if he had held back from launching his invading force and had attacked solely from the air. A great victory by the Luftwaffe over the Royal Air Force might well have been decisive and settled the whole war; with undisputed command of the air the German army and navy would at least have found their task easier. As it was, the Luftwaffe was very seriously hampered by the necessity of maintaining air cover over the beaches; that was a ball and chain attached to the ankle of the Luftwaffe, hampering its freedom of action at every turn; the first radio message sent by Von Rundstedt from Rye was a demand for air cover, and Hitler, with his armour poised no more than sixty miles from London, was bound to insist on Goering's meeting that demand.

Already by the end of that first day Fighter Command had been able to evolve a pattern, a plan of action, which promised victory provided the strength of the Luftwaffe was not too overwhelming. With radar and by the aid of the Observer Corps it was possible to estimate with reasonable certainty the strength of the German air cover, and by radio-telephone it was comparatively easy to launch superior forces of fighters at moments when that air cover was at a low figure and while radar could assure Fighter

Command that no German reinforcements could arrive for twenty minutes at least. So, technically and tactically and strategically, Fighter Command held important advantages, while the battle raged with an intensity and a ferocity unprecedented in the history of air warfare. Indeed, if night had not put an end to it, the battle must have reached a lull very soon from the sheer exhaustion of the pilots and crews.

So night came down, affording a little leisure to Fighter Command to draw up a balance sheet, to count up losses in pilots and in machines, to revise earlier estimates of German losses, to issue orders for the resting of the pilots – on this, almost the shortest night of the year – and to move down reinforcements of personnel and material from the areas which clearly were no longer threatened. Night came down, while it was still afternoon in New York, upon a breathless and sleeping world, while governments from Lima to Tokyo studied the innumerable bulletins that had been issued. 'The Admiralty regrets to announce . . .'; 'The Air Ministry announces . . .'; 'Berlin reports that . . .' Those governments were trying to weigh the possibilities of victory one way or the other; what was in the balance was the destiny of humanity.

It was in the afternoon of July 1, 1940, that the British navy made visual contact with the German navy, and the Battle of the North Foreland began – the battle of ship against ship, that is to say. Ships had fought submarines, and ships had fought planes; planes had fought planes, and mines laid days or weeks earlier had taken their toll all through that long day. But at three P.M. a lookout in the British destroyer screen suddenly saw through his binoculars the distant masts as the German ships came out of a patch of slight mist.

'There they are,' he said to himself, and yelled his report.

'There they are,' said the British admiral to his chief of staff three minutes later – at the very same second as Admiral Lütjens on the bridge of the *Scharnhorst* said, 'There they are' to himself. The guns were already firing;

this was no Jutland, when each side had dozens of capital ships to bring into action. On the German side there were only three, even including the pocket battleship *Lützow* fresh from her defeat of the British destroyers, fighting today in line with the battle cruisers *Scharnhorst* and *Gneisenau*. On the British side there were six, *Rodney* and *Hood*, *Repulse* and *Nelson*, *Royal Sovereign* and *Ramillies*. Deployment was instant, unlike at Jutland. Nor was the mist as hampering; this time the visibility was almost good. And, unlike Jutland, the tactical and strategical situations were such as to bring about close and decisive action.

Neither side had much room to manoeuvre – in fact, examination of the charted minefields off the Kentish and Belgian coasts leaves the student impressed at the temerity of the opposing admirals in engaging at all. But Lütjens had to fight. His mission was to delay the entrance of British naval forces into the Strait of Dover, and the British navy had only to push on to compel him to give action – especially with Hitler sending signal after signal, each demanding action. In those conditions, against odds of two to one in capital ships and five to one in destroyers, Lütjens' fate was sealed; his destruction was certain before the battle began, unless some extraordinary factor altered the balance.

For a moment early in the battle it seemed as if some such factor might indeed be present, when the *Hood* blew up while the first salvos were being exchanged. To this day there is a certain body of opinion which attributes the loss of the *Hood* to a chance contact with a mine, and not – as is usually held – to an eleven-inch shell from the *Scharnhorst* which found its way to the magazines through a structural defect. The appalling loss might well have daunted a man of less tough fibre than the British admiral, but, as it was, the sixteen-inch guns of the *Rodney*, admirably served, were already winning the battle; Lütjens may have even been already dead at the moment when the *Hood* blew up.

The *Scharnhorst* and *Gneisenau* displayed the remarkable capacity to take punishment which had distinguished German ships since they were first constructed, but from early in the battle they were hardly better than floating targets as a result of the damage done to their fire-control apparatus by the British salvos. The attack by the British destroyers, well timed and not to be evaded, because of the proximity of the Belgian minefields, hastened the end. The *Scharnhorst*, it is believed, took no less than seven torpedoes before she sank on an even keel in the shallows, so that her battered upper works were left awash at low water.

It was a battle of annihilation, as the circumstances made inevitable; the interposition of the German navy had not prolonged the brief German command of the straits by more than three hours at the cost of these frightful losses.

Meanwhile, far down the Channel, a desperate series of minor actions had been fought. Here the two German light cruisers and the other half of the German U-boats had endeavoured to delay the advance eastward of the British forces, gathered in from the Western Approaches. Again it was a battle of annihilation, this time almost of mutual annihilation, for the losses suffered by the British navy, despite the superiority of numbers which they enjoyed here, were very severe indeed. The fighting was as confused as might be expected where submarines intervened in an action between surface craft and where the opposing air forces were continually launching surprise attacks.

The *Nürnberg* sank off Beachy Head; the *Emden* went down while struggling to reach the shelter of Cherbourg, but three British light cruisers joined them on the wreck-littered bottom of the English Channel, and two more only with difficulty managed to limp into the protected waters of The Solent. But even so, that left eleven British destroyers to dominate the surface, and in a series of fierce actions they were able to hunt down the U-boats – the shallow Channel with its numerous minefields was no place for submarines on the defensive. The Channel tides, coursing first east and then west, left the coasts of England and France greasy with the oil that welled up from the sunken ships and dotted with the corpses of the men who died.

And like the tides, the British light forces swept into the Channel from the east and from the west, and that night was made vivid by a hundred minor actions as the German small craft fought to the death, motorboats and torpedo boats and minesweepers opposing a crushing superiority of destroyers and light cruisers. The *Fritz Reuter* was caught, just before dawn, before she had completed her second trip to England – and she came nearer to doing so than most of the unfortunate river craft employed in that luckless venture. Few enough left the invasion beaches at all; the *Fritz Reuter* actually returned to Calais, loaded herself with troops again and headed back for Rye. But seven miles from Dungeness the fat captain, nodding over his wheel as he struggled against sleep, was roused to full wakefulness as a star shell burst overhead, illuminating the *Fritz Reuter* and the water around her with a hard, relentless glare. That was the last he saw as shells at point-blank range came crashing into the frail sides of the *Fritz Reuter*. He was dead before those sides had opened and let in the sea upon the screaming soldiers crammed in the holds.

Once more it must be stressed that these naval actions, important though they were, and effectively though they sealed the fate of the German landing forces, were not necessarily the vital factor in the brief campaign. The air battle began again at dawn over the beaches, to continue through the long and desperate day; if the RAF had been defeated in that air battle, the history of the world might have been different. The military experts to this day argue about every aspect of the campaign. There are many who think that if Hitler had not made his attempt at invasion, but had massed the Luftwaffe for an all-out attack upon

England sometime in August, 1940, he might have overborne the RAF by sheer weight of numbers, English radar and the defensive attitude notwithstanding. That is a point which can never be settled, but at least it is agreed that the need to provide air cover for the invasion beaches imposed a decisive disadvantage on the Luftwaffe.

In Fighter Command they tried as best they could to take the measure of the situation. The war could be won or lost in the air, and if it were to be won, it would be the fighters that would win it. So the arduous day went on, and fresh figures were added to the revised balance sheets. The dwindling numbers of British fighter planes and fighter pilots could be counted by all who were in on the secret. The German losses could be guessed at with fair accuracy, the German reserves only between the wide limits of optimism and pessimism. There were crashed German fighters to be counted all over the southern counties between the invasion beaches and the Midlands, but within the ten-mile perimeter held by Von Rundstedt there were many more, not so easy to count; we know now that in those eighty square miles no fewer than three hundred German fighters lay wrecked in the fields and coppices, and a hundred British fighters along with them. The reconnaissance planes could report that there was hardly a field without its wreck, piled among the abandoned parachutes.

Fighter Command could only continue as they had begun, accumulating successive striking forces and launching them to the attack at the moments when the reports of the Observer Corps and the radar observers indicated favourable opportunities. During the decisive day of July first there were no fewer than fifteen of these attacks delivered and, as nearly as can be judged from the defective German records, more than half of these delivered with a numerical superiority of at least three to one, and never once without some small superiority. The occasions when the numbers were nearly even were those when German reinforcements had flown in low over the Channel

196

and were not reported to Fighter Command until it was too late to recall the attack.

There were at least six distinct periods when the air over the invasion beaches was practically clear of the Luftwaffe, and there were four heavy raids launched by Bomber Command in consequence.

The pace was too hot to last. Fighter Command, hoarding its dwindling forces and listening to the anxious reports from wing and from group regarding the fatigue of the pilots, was compelled to keep a considerable reserve in hand in readiness both for some unforeseen move by the Germans and for the final battle when the German land forces should advance. But the Luftwaffe was in worse condition still. To maintain even a quarter of its numbers over the invasion beaches meant no rest at all for any of its fighters; to maintain less than that exposed them to the attack of superior numbers of Spitfires and Hurricanes. The periods when the beaches were left without air cover grew longer and longer, and there was Bomber Command awaiting those moments with the planes fuelled and armed and less than half an hour's flight from the beaches.

A sort of rhythm soon appeared in the battle, a pulsation; a wave of German fighters would appear and then ebb away; the bombers would strike, and then too late a fresh wave of German fighters would appear. We know now, comparing the records of the RAF with the war diary of the German high command, that this rhythm was not fortuitous; the bomber attacks called forth the wildest protests from Von Rundstedt, and these protests, reaching Hitler, brought sharp reprimands upon Goering, and Goering, against his better judgement and to the despair of his staff, was compelled to make fresh demands on his fighter pilots. The memoirs of half a dozen German officers tell of the shifts and subterfuges into which Goering was forced during that dreadful day; his attempts to delay the departure of each fighter force, the lies he told regarding their strength, and his pleadings with the *Führer*, while the losses grew unbearable, for a slackening of the pace.

The climax came with two stunning blows delivered by Fighter Command in the evening. In each case Fighter Command received early warning of the assembly of the German fighters over the French coast and was able to gather superior forces in readiness, high up and with the westering sun behind them. Those two battles have come to be known as the 'six-o'clock battle' and the 'eight-thirty battle'; and we have a vivid picture in the memoirs of Von Rangsdorf of the effect of the second upon Goering.

The fact that that action was begun was known at once at Luftwaffe headquarters, but the reports that next came in were as fragmentary as may be imagined, although sufficient to arouse apprehension. Then came in reports of German fighters in flight across the Channel with Spitfires in hot pursuit, and then came in the first reports from the airfields in France as the survivors landed. These all told of losses, but the planes continued to come in, ten, twenty, thirty of them, some with pilots wounded and the planes shot up, but at least while they came in there was reason to hope for more. But they ceased to arrive, and the minutes ticked by, until the limit of fuel endurance was reached and it was plain that no more could arrive.

The Luftwaffe staff stood silent, watching Goering, as he gradually brought himself to accept the fact that he had sent out two hundred fighter planes and that only thirty had returned. That force was the last scraping of the barrel. One thousand German fighter planes had been destroyed since the invasion began. Goering would have to tell Hitler that the battle was lost, that the RAF had secured command of the air; it was obvious to all who watched that from Goering's point of view the important fact was that his own position and prestige were imperilled by the necessity of admitting that his boastings had come to naught and his prevarications during the day revealed.

It is interesting that the moment Goering chose to make

198

these revelations followed immediately upon the news of the annihilation of the German navy at the Battle of the North Foreland and provoked the historic scene which several diarists have recorded. Hitler indulged himself in a burst of frantic rage. He sneered at his navy for its incompetence, at his army for its sluggishness, and at Goering and the Luftwaffe for their lack of resolution. He was utterly determined to fight the battle to the bitter end; the alternative, of tamely admitting defeat and abandoning Von Rundstedt to his fate, was something he could not contemplate for a moment. He was convinced, despite all the evidence to the contrary, that England was on the brink of surrender. Another resolute effort would bring her down; it was only a question of firmness of will. Hence his violent orders, to Goering to scrape together pilots and planes from every corner of Europe and to continue to give Von Rundstedt air support, and to Von Rundstedt to assemble every man that could march and to strike a blow at London without regard for his own shortcomings.

We have Von Rundstedt's own account of the next day's fighting from the German side. There can be no denying that he did all that man could do, more than most generals would have found possible. He had sorted out his disordered army into units and had established a chain of command; he had improvised thirty batteries of artillery and by one means or another he had made them mobile. He had assembled two sets of bridging equipment out of the incredible muddle and had made them mobile too. He was in complete agreement for once with Hitler regarding the necessity for striking an immediate blow, because, as he points out, there was no possibility of receiving a single ton more of supplies or another battalion from France; his army would never be stronger, whereas the British opposing him would grow stronger every hour. So he was able to answer Hitler's furious messages with the calm reply that he was moving up his forces that night ready to attack.

This was indeed true. The beaches which Bomber Command were pounding all through the night were practically deserted as we know now. Von Rundstedt left a mass of miscellaneous supplies there, including a considerable amount of artillery ammunition, from sheer lack of transport. He moved up his four divisions – brigade groups would be a better description of them – along the dark roads and lanes to Broad Oak and Beckley, putting almost literally every man he had into the fighting line, abandoning the rest of his perimeter. He had a hundred tanks; he had petrol and ammunition for a single day's fighting. His deployment was admirably managed even during the dark hours, and at dawn on July second he struck his blow, and the thin screen of British troops along the line of the Rother was shattered instantly into fragments.

In all England at that moment there were seventy-five infantry tanks fit for service, but there were forty cruiser tanks and no fewer than five hundred light tanks. The driving force of the government and the admirable co-operation of the railways managed to make almost all this armour available for battle on July second. During the night when Von Rundstedt was affecting his deployment, the First Armoured Division, battle-hardened and admirably trained, was already assembling at Tonbridge, and the Second Armoured, having completed its complex railway journey, was in touch and detraining at Horsmonden and Goudhurst, an arrangement since criticised as a deployment too far forward, luckily without too disastrous results. There were five infantry divisions in support, deploying along the main-line railway to Ashford. As regards mortars and anti-tank guns, they were almost entirely deficient, but they had two hundred field guns between them and three hundred rounds for each – more guns and twice as much ammunition as Von Rundstedt could boast.

Telephones were ringing wildly that morning at Sandhurst and Hawkhurst, Tenterden and Cranbrook, as devoted volunteers along the Rother reported the German advance; more than once the messages were cut short abruptly, and the listeners at the other end could hear the sound of shots coming over the wires from the dangling instruments, beneath which the speakers who had telephoned now lay in their blood. Those lovely lanes of Kent and East Sussex, beautiful in the level light of dawn, echoed to the rumble of the German armour. Parties of German infantry, pushing forward with cautious haste, left wide tracks over the dewy meadows of the Rother Valley.

Newenden fell almost at once, pinched out by turning columns to right and left. But Bodiam Castle stood a siege – the first for centuries, where a desperate garrison held out behind the thick walls, sheltered from the armour by the moat on which the water lilies bloomed in their summer loveliness. The garrison, however, could do nothing to hinder the repair of the bridge, and the small forces at the main road bridge at Udiam could do little more. Once over the river the German forces could roll vigorously forward. Now there were diverging lanes and tracks by which strongpoints could be turned and isolated and attacked from the rear; the general newly in command of the German armour could display his talents in his bold handling of his columns. That was how Sandhurst was taken, by a thrust to the rear from Sandhurst Cross, although the volunteers there fought to the last in defence of their homes, as the volunteers did in so many places.

The loss of Hawkhurst is not so easily explained, for it was held by two battalions of regular troops from good regiments. But they apparently were mishandled, and paid with their lives for their general's mistake; as the general in question met the same fate it is perhaps best not to enquire further. Certain it is that the news of the capture of Hawkhurst, which reached headquarters in London at four in the afternoon, produced a most disturbing effect. We know now that the decision was very nearly reached to let loose Bomber Command upon the invaders with the stores of poison gas accumulated in the country as a precaution in case Hitler were ever to use it. Luckily it was decided to wait a little longer, so that England was saved from the odium of having initiated poison-gas warfare, and the weapon remained unused.

Within a few minutes the situation cleared. Constant air reconnaissance, carried out with ease in the absence of German air cover and the almost complete absence of German anti-aircraft artillery, at last brought conviction as to the weakness – unbelievable until now – of the German forces. First and Second Armoured divisions began to come into action, the first clash of armour taking place in the extremely difficult tank country between Hawkhurst and Flimwell; the road there is a defile hemmed in by extensive wooded areas in which the headlong German attack was easily checked. There was a whole British infantry division to defend Cranbrook by now, and the attack launched by Von Rundstedt there with two brigade groups and an armoured battalion was beaten back before nightfall.

'The fact remains,' said the American news commentator that night in New York, 'that there is still a German army on British soil. It does not seem to have advanced very far, but Berlin is emphatic about the capture of numbers of prisoners, and perhaps tomorrow may see London in grave danger. On the other hand it seems quite certain that, despite the loss of the *Hood*, the Royal Navy has destroyed the German fleet and has regained command of the Channel. And if the Air Ministry claim that two thousand four hundred German planes have been destroyed during the present fighting is anywhere near correct, then the Luftwaffe has lost command of the air and Von Rundstedt is cut off from all supply and reinforcement. We can only wait and see.'

The commentator was speaking at ten o'clock at night in New York. It was early in the morning in England, and already in those dark hours before dawn the troops were moving up and deploying for the day's battle. Von Rundstedt was dozing uncomfortably in the tent that his staff had set up for him in Iden Wood, a mile or two out of Rye. This was his command headquarters, hidden among the trees, for he had no desire at all that another bombing attack should bring about another involuntary change of command of the invading forces. There was a constant droning of planes overhead to disturb his sleep and to warn his wakeful chief of staff of this imminent possibility. As the birds began their first song the first messages began to come in from the units at the front, and with the first light the battle exploded.

The heavy tanks fought out their battle in a slogging match that ranged from Hurst Green to Goudhurst – it was within sight of Goudhurst Station that a British field-gun battery knocked out the three German tanks which advanced nearer to London than any other part of the German forces. The figures as ascertained now make it clear that the Germans were outnumbered here, where eighty-one tanks engaged sixty-five Germans in a battle of mutual annihilation while the infantry forces fought it out along the line extending eastward from Cranbrook. The German tanks gave a good account of themselves despite the frightful handicap of constant air attack; the German infantry held fast throughout the morning against the converging attacks delivered upon them. It was a brigade of cruiser tanks that broke the deadlock, turning the German left flank by a sudden advance from Battle.

When the heavy armour was all engaged, the light armour could sweep forward unchecked, so that all Kent became a cauldron of action, friends and foes intermingled. The scanty German reserves fought desperately – we have only today to look at the ruined remains of Brede village to see how desperately – but the numerical odds against them were overwhelming; the eight British divisions which ultimately took part in the battle outnumbered the German infantry by nearly three to one. At noon Von Rundstedt knew he had lost the battle.

At four o'clock in the afternoon a BBC announcer's calm voice came on the air. 'We interrupt our programme to bring you the news that Colonel-General Von Rundstedt, commanding the Nazi forces in England, has just been made prisoner by our light armoured forces. The fighting continues.'

It was the evening of the next day that the prime minister made his historic speech. 'An hour ago the last organised unit of the Nazi army in England made its surrender among the ruins of Rye. There are still scattered German soldiers hiding from our forces in the woods and fields of Kent and Sussex. Their lives will be spared, and I call upon the Local Defence Volunteers to be merciful, however justified they may think they are in exacting vengeance for our burned villages and slaughtered civilians. Let us reserve our vengeance for Hitler and the guttersnipe crew who surround him. Today they know the first taste of defeat, and that is a taste with which they will become more and more familiar in the days to come.'

It has been remarked over and over again that the defeat of the Invasion of Britain was the turning-point of the war, but it will do no harm to stress this statement again; it will be of advantage, in addition, to indicate how the battle was of such importance. Perhaps the most important consequence was the one least susceptible to exact definition – the moral effect. It was Hitler's first failure, and it was no small one; it was something that could not possibly be covered up or excused after the fanfare of publicity with which it was initiated by Göebbels. There was a negative importance too; as long as invasion was only threatened and not attempted, no one could be sure of its failure. It might succeed, and England might be overthrown. That possibility could have bolstered up for some time Hitler's prestige at the dizzy height to which it was raised by the conquest of France; as it was, the failure more than nullified the preceding success, and contributed enormously to Hitler's rapid decline in the face of the subsequent military disasters.

These latter stemmed, of course, directly from the defeat. The enormous losses in the air robbed Germany of most of her military potential. It is noteworthy that by the invasion date Britain was already building faster than Germany in the air, and the swing of the pendulum was naturally very wide. It was England's overwhelming air superiority that made the reconquest of Norway in the spring of 1941 so comparatively easy; the German garrisons in Norway were, as a result of England's superiority by sea and air, as isolated from each other as if they had been stationed on as many different islands and they were easily reduced, one by one. The loss of Norway, of Swedish iron and – just as important – of the command of the Baltic sealed Hitler's fate.

The losses of the German army – elements of a few divisions – during the invasion were practically negligible save for the moral effect, but the naval losses were of the greatest importance. Three-quarters of the German naval personnel were killed, drowned or captured; three-quarters of the German U-boats were destroyed. Had it not been for these losses, it is conceivable that Hitler might have built up his U-boat force to constitute a serious threat to British sea communications by 1941, and certainly by 1942; as it was, he had too few seeds left to grow a large crop. Incidentally, his surface navy, if it had survived, would have been a powerful auxiliary in such a campaign. As it was, he had too small a force left to permit any serious expansion, and the denial of the Baltic to the U-boats as a training area put the capping stone on his difficulties in this direction.

The destruction of so much – estimates run as high as eighty-five per cent – of Germany's inland shipping is another factor to be taken into account. Even by the time the invasion was launched, the mere withdrawal of that tonnage had done serious harm to Germany's internal economy, and despite Hitler's desperate attempts to replace it – efforts that had an important bearing on his whole armament programmes – the situation was never stabilised before the end came. The crippling local shortages that contributed so much to the disillusionment of the German people would hardly have developed. In sum, it is hard to escape the conclusion that Hitler's decision to attempt the invasion was most important in shortening the war and hastening his own destruction.

A selection of bestselling Adventure/Thriller Fiction from Sphere Books

A selection of Bestsellers from Sphere Books

SARGASSO	Edwin Corley	95p	☐
RAISE THE TITANIC!	Clive Cussler	95p	☐
STORY OF MY LIFE	Moshe Dayan	£1.50p	☐
THE HAB THEORY	Allan W. Eckert	£1.50p	☐
THE CRASH OF '79	Paul Erdman	95p	☐
EMMA AND I	Sheila Hocken	85p	☐
UNTIL THE COLOURS FADE	Tim Jeal	£1.50p	☐
DR JOLLY'S BOOK OF CHILDCARE			
	Dr Hugh Jolly	£1.95p	☐
MAJESTY	Robert Lacey	£1.95p	☐
STAR WARS	George Lucas	95p	☐
NIGHTRUNNERS OF BENGAL	John Masters	65p	☐
THE CHINESE ULTIMATUM			
	Edward McGhee & Robin Moore	95p	☐
THE MITTENWALD SYNDICATE	Frederick Nolan	95p	☐
NORTH CAPE	Joe Poyer	85p	☐
THE RUSSIANS	Hedrick Smith	£1.50p	☐
CLOSE ENCOUNTERS OF THE THIRD KIND			
	Steven Spielberg	85p	☐
A MAN CALLED INTREPID	William Stevenson	£1.25p	☐
STAR FIRE	Ingo Swann	£1.25p	☐
FIREFOX	Craig Thomas	95p	☐
RUIN FROM THE AIR			
	Gordon Thomas & Max Morgan Witts	£1.50p	☐
FADE-OUT	Patrick Tilley	95p	☐

All Sphere books are available at your local bookshop or newsagent, or can be ordered direct from the publisher. Just tick the titles you want and fill in the form below.

Name ....

Address ....

....

Write to Sphere Books, Cash Sales Department, P.O. Box 11, Falmouth, Cornwall TR10 9EN

Please enclose cheque or postal order to the value of the cover price plus:

UK: 22p for the first book plus 10p per copy for each additional book ordered to a maximum charge of 82p

OVERSEAS: 30p for the first book and 10p for each additional book

BFPO and EIRE: 22p for the first book plus 10p per copy for the next 6 books, thereafter 4p per book

Sphere Books reserve the right to show new retail prices on covers which may differ from those previously advertised in the text or elsewhere, and to increase postal rates in accordance with the GPO.